Anonymous

Miller Henry

Minister of the German Reformed Church

Anonymous

Miller Henry
Minister of the German Reformed Church

ISBN/EAN: 9783337297633

Printed in Europe, USA, Canada, Australia, Japan

Cover: Foto ©Raphael Reischuk / pixelio.de

More available books at **www.hansebooks.com**

MEMOIRS

OF

MISS HENRIETTA B. MILLER

LATE TEACHER OF FAIRVIEW SCHOOL,

WHO DIED AT

WAYNESBORO, PENNA.

DECEMBER 23, 1874.

THE AMIABLE FRIEND. THE ADVOCATE OF EDUCATION.
THE MODEL TEACHER. THE REAL CHRISTIAN.

WAYNESBORO, PA.
PUBLISHED BY THE AUTHOR.
1877.

Dedicated

TO THE MEMBERS OF THE

Franklin County Teachers' Institute;

AS A GRATEFUL

ACKNOWLEDGMENT OF THE ENCOMIUM ON HER LIFE,

PASSED BY THE INSTITUTE

ONE YEAR AFTER HER DEATH.

PREFACE.

To record the achievements of illustrious statesmen or valiant heroes would be patriotic and win applause; but to record the early culture of a bright-eyed little girl, and show how she was nurtured in childhood, and how her mind was gradually expanded and matured, as well as the growth of the body, until she became an object of admiration and qualified for extensive usefulness, may serve as examples to those who have the instruction of youth, and prove a greater blessing to society than a recital of the heroic deeds of warriors and statesmen.

The Bible says, " The righteous shall be held in everlasting remembrance," and it is incumbent to preserve the incidents of a use-

ful life and of a happy death, for the benefit
of those who may come after us.

Such considerations influenced the writer of
the following pages, which are dedicated to
the members of the Franklin County Teachers' Institute, with whom the subject of the
memoirs associated several years with much
cordiality, and for whose interest she manifested a special regard, and whose annual
meeting she attended within three weeks of
her death.

CONTENTS.

—

CHAPTER I.

PAGE.

Parentage and place of Nativity—Early Life at
Troy—Death of Two Sisters—Removal to Tur-
butville......... 9

CHAPTER II.

Early Fondness for Reading—Home Training—
Importance of Parental Instruction and Example—A Mother's Influence............................ 16

CHAPTER III.

Removal to Chulasky—Benevolent Enterprise of
Samuel R. Wood, etc..................................... 28

CHAPTER IV.

Rapid Intellectual Development—Proficiency in
Music—Interest in Sabbath-school and Religious
Literature—Systematic Bible Reading............. 47

CHAPTER V.

Removal to Phœnixville—Joins German Reform-
ed Church—Enters Linden Cottage Seminary—
Removal to Adamstown—Becomes a Teacher—
Removal to Waynesboro, etc........ 56

8 CONTENTS.

CHAPTER VI.

PAGE.

Failing Health—Christmas Festival—Last Illness
—Not Afraid to Die—Dying to Live Again—
Funeral Serv ices.. 67

CHAPTER VII.

Tributes to Her Memory—Resolution of Teachers'
Institute—Letters of Condolence—Death of Two
of her Friends—Dying Words of Pious Women
—Love for the Dead—Early Intellectual Development the Result of Parental Care 81

CHAPTER VIII.

Training of Children—Study of Languages—Val-
ue of Elementary Instruction—Growth of the
Scholastic Profession—Rewards of the Faithful
Teacher,... 98

MISCELLANEOUS ADDENDA.

Paternal Care—Studies Suitable for Young Ladies
—Works to be Read—Miss Miller's Favorite
Hymns and Poems——Alice Cary's Dying
Hymn.................................109–169

MEMOIR

OF

MISS HENRIETTA B. MILLER.

———•———

CHAPTER I.

Parentage and Place of Nativity—Early life at Troy—
Death of Two Sisters—Removal to Turbutville.

MISS HENRIETTA BREWSTER MIL-
LER was the third daughter of the Rev.
Henry and Sarah T. Miller. The first two
daughters, Victoria and Vandalia, were born
at Tarlton, Pickaway county, Ohio; the former
in 1838, the latter in 1841, while their father
was minister of the German Reformed Church
of that place. Owing to providential occurrences in the family, Mr. M. was induced to
relinquish his charge in 1841, and to return
to the place of the nativity of Mrs. M., at

Troy, Bradford county, Pa., that she might have the care of two sisters whose health had failed beyond the prospect of recovery; and where, in a pleasant rural abode, Mr. M. would find a home congenial to literary pursuits; and especially favorable, on account of its healthfulness and beautiful surroundings, whereat to rear those first-born lovely little girls—the joy of fond parents, the embodiment of health, beauty and loveliness.

The long journey of five hundred miles was performed in a one-horse carriage. The high hills had not then been brought low, nor little valleys exalted by the construction of railroads, or cars conveyed by the iron-horse at rapid speed, as now. Hence three weeks were consumed by steady, patient toil over mountain, hill and dale, which, by a propitious providence, was successfully accomplished, all in good health, without any accident to mar the enjoyment of the journey. Having thus returned to the home of Mrs. M.'s youth, to the joy of her aged mother and her sisters, there was much to flatter the anticipation of a pleasant abode.   As month glided after month, enhancing attachment to the place, and brightening prospects for the future, nothing added to the delights of home so much as those pledges of heaven—those two little cherubs, that by their peculiar sprightliness attracted the admiration of all who saw them.

But, alas, how uncertain are the events of life !

How often the fond hopes of parents are cross'd !
How oft the bud is nipt by the frost,
When those which are cherished, and dearly beloved,
Are transplanted to bloom in the garden above !

The scarlet fever became epidemic.   Each of these little girls encountered a virulent attack that baffled the skill of two eminent physicians, with the best of nursing.   They both fell victims; and on the day that completed the year of starting on the journey from Tarlton, Vandalia was borne to the silent grave!

Victoria survived eleven days, when her mortal remains were deposited there likewise, on June 16, 1842.

They were strongly attached to each other while living, and were not long separated by death.

A marble tablet, with appropriate inscription, marks the place of their repose in the cemetery one mile east of Troy—

> Yet, again we hope to meet them,
>> When the days of life are fled;
> There, in heaven, with joy to greet them,
>> Where no farewell tear is shed.

Thus, a house was left desolate, and other bereavements, in quick succession, followed, until, in the course of six years, Mrs. M.'s mother, two sisters, a brother, and other relatives, with intimate friends of the vicinity, were called to their eternal home!

But amidst these chequered scenes of joy and grief, there was one more added to the family.

Henrietta, the subject of this narrative, was born January 25, 1847, and became the object of strong attachment and regard, and seemed to be a pledge of happy days to come.

Perhaps there is no situation more unstable than that of a minister of the gospel; being frequently induced to change localities for professional considerations, or subject to the fluctuations of the times, impelled by prospects of greater good.

Hence, while pursuing this narrative, we will follow the family through several removals. From Troy to Turbutville, in 1848; thence to Chulasky, in 1850; back to Turbutville, in 1852; thence to Shirleysburg, in 1858; thence to Phœnixville, in 1861; thence to Adamstown, in 1867; and finally to Waynesboro, in 1872. Mr. M. was offered some property as a residence in Turbutville, and induced to move there with the view of establishing a select school. The inducements were not very flattering, but the wants were evident.

The village then consisted of twenty-nine tenements, nearly all frame buildings, that had been erected in the early part of the present century; with an old log church that would seat about 300 persons, owned conjointly by the German Reformed and Lutherans, and occupied by each on successive Sabbaths with a German sermon; each of which had about 200 communicant members, kept up according to the common custom of the Germans, of catechising the youth annually, and confirming as many of the catechumens as were deemed worthy.

There was at the time no other house of worship in all that township, though remarkably wealthy; and a part of which not inappropriately called *Paradise*, *with* ADAM *and* EVE *living in it.* A venerable pair, Adam Schuyler and his wife Eve. It was rarely the case that there was an English sermon preached there, and no meetings at night. An attempt had been made to have a singing school at night; but it was so much annoyed by the rowdies that they were obliged to meet in the office of the 'Squire of the town.

Where there was so little light of the gospel, it would hardly be expected to find much liberality in patronizing a select school; and yet even there, there were individuals who expressed a special desire for such. Mr. M., accordingly, fitted up a building adjoining his residence for the purpose, and made the experiment, which was well received and tolerably well patronized. The place has much improved since then, containing three times as many inhabitants now, with four spacious brick churches, and the preaching all in English—except, occasionally, in German.

CHAPTER II.

Ear'y Fondness for Reading—Home Training—Importance of Parental Instruction and Example—A Mother's Influence.

HERE Henrietta became familiar with the exercises of the school-room. Being adjacent to the dwelling, and under the fostering care of parents who cherished solicitude for her welfare, she imbibed a fondness for books that aided her in the acquisition of knowledge. She learned to read when not more than four years old, and at five years she astonished superior judges by the accuracy of her reading.

Some may startle at the thought of having a child learn to read so young, and conjecture that the discipline must have been rigid, or that she must have been possessed of extraordinary talents. With regard to the first, it is

asserted there was nothing rigid, and no harshness employed. *The ways of wisdom are ways
of pleasantness, and all her paths are paths of
peace.*

It is a mistake to suppose that harshness or
severity is necessary or admissible, either in
the nursery or in the school-room. Those
parents or teachers who practice either will
never thus make good scholars nor philanthropists. On the other hand, impartial observation will show that it is gentleness and kindness, with judicious system and uniformity,
that is needed in the cultivation and training
of the youthful mind.

It is not claimed that she was possessed of
any extraordinary talents—although her intellectual faculties ranked very high. But it
was owing to the wise, seasonable and kind
parental attention that every parent might
practice with equal happy results, that developed her faculties, qualified her for usefulness,

and secured for her so much honor and admiration.   It is said that Martin Luther's
mother taught him the ten commandments
and the Lord's prayer from the tiles on the
fire-place, and so did the mother of Dr. Dod-
ridge, while they were quite small; and yet
that early culture did not make dull boys or
them; but rather, by giving an early start to
the growth of their minds before their intellects were stultified by indolence and gross
habits, the intellectual gained an ascendency
over the bodily faculties, and they became re-
nowned for the vigor of their minds and for
their superior intelligence and piety.

Experience and observation has shown that
it is easier to train up a child right, than to
train it up wrong; or, according to Solomon's injunction, "Train up a child in the
way he should go and when he is old, he will
not depart from it."

Those who train up children according to

Christian culture and the improved methods of modern plans of governing schools, receive the divine assistance and the cordial sanction of the pupils. The child will appreciate kind instruction, and will become enraptured with intellectual rather than with bodily exercises, and thus make ample returns for all attention given to it, and God will bless the effort.

Never was there a cross word or angry look given to Henrietta. Hence as Paul said to Timothy, "From a child thou hast known the Holy Scriptures;" so, from the early instruction kindly communicated at the family altar, she soon showed much of the character of the real Christian, being amiable in deportment, and upright and noble in all her aspirations. Never, from childhood, was she averse to obey her parents, but always manifested a cordial compliance with their instruction. And thus a mutual delight was experienced both by the parent or teacher and the pupil. The teacher delighted to teach the pupil, and that pupil delighted to be taught.

As in the case of Milton, who said, "When I was yet a child few childish plays to me were pleasing; but I ever was intent to learn and know, and do some useful thing;" so with Henrietta, she was not so much fascinated with levity as with rational conviviality or with true rational cheerfulness; and accomplished more during her short life than others have in many years. Turning from boisterous mirth, she gave a preference to the sedative and intellectual, instead of the romp or lounge. She passed her time in acquiring knowledge, or industriously performing some useful part, and seldom passed an hour that was not usefully and honorably employed. Hence she usually attracted the attention and won the esteem of the better classes, especially of those who were her seniors in years.

Here we pause in our narrative, to state

that the education of children depends mainly on the mother. Hence the Rev. James Patterson, Capt. John Newton, Henry Martin, Col. Gardiner, and many other distinguished men, acknowledged that they owed their conversion and all their eminence to the early instruction of their mothers. If mothers were judicious and faithful in their attentions to their children, they might early give such direction to their habits as greatly to alleviate their anxieties, and find them a source of real gladness from childhood, rather than worriment, grief and shame through life. The mother who neglects her child until it is impelled by weariness and the suffering impulses of nature, will thus make it fretful and turbulent. It will become disobedient and resentful, and thus occasion much discomfort during its childhood, and shame and sorrow in its mature years. If the proper moral and mental culture of children is neglected by parents,

the devil and wicked men will very likely effect their ruin. By the neglect of parents,
the dispositions of children become perverted
and the faculties of their minds greatly im-
paired.

Thus we learn the importance of mothers
especially giving kind maternal and cheerful attention to their children from early childhood :
Professor Wickersham has said the best part of
education is given before the child is five years
old. By this we don't mean silly dalliance, or
stuffing them with sweetmeats. We think
children, as well as adults, should be treated
rationally, as rational beings; and to treat
them (as some do) in a silly, babyish manner,
will make simpletons, and not wise and good
persons of them. To feed them too much
confectionery, is like allowing men to use too
much whiskey, while experience has shown
that it is better to take none at all, except
as medicine, when really needed. But the

mother who anticipates the wants and reliefs of her infant, who promptly approaches it with cheerful looks and kind words, will soon find how cordially it responds in like manner. It will thus learn to wait patiently, and as reason becomes developed, how cheerfully it will obey through love!

On the other hand, to worry a child by long neglect, and then to terrify it with angry looks, or threats, or blows, the intellect will be stunted, and it will grow up to be a scourge rather than a comfort to those who bore it.

Every mother should sing lullabys, with hymns of devotion and familiar instruction, to her children. "Music hath charms to soothe the troubled breast;" and it is remarkable how soon and how accurately children learn to sing—and what a tranquilizing influence on their lives!

There should likewise be an organ, melodeon, or some other musical instrument, in every house.   As a general rule, a musical family is a happy family.

No discord nor envy found

Where music sends its cheerful sound.

Every mother should teach each of her children to read before it is five years old.   It is a shame to think how this is neglected.   Some say it is too much trouble; but they take trouble to adorn their bodies by dressing them handsomely, and is not the soul of more worth than the body, and shall there be less attention given to the immortal spirit than to the perishing body?   Some mothers say they have no time to teach their children to read and sing, or to teach them the catechism, and yet find time to gossip and to lounge.   To such we would frankly say, if they neglect and suffer their children to grow up in ignorance and sin they may have to take time to mourn over their vices before they grow old.

While we thus particularly set forth the duty

of the mother to give proper attention to her children, we do not wish to be understood to exempt the father from responsibility. We know there are peculiar and special duties of each, and mutual duties in which each should participate. The father as well as the mother is in duty bound to give much personal attention to the culture and training of their children. He should co-operate with the mother in giving instruction, and in practicing and advancing them in what the mother has taught them. And it is especially the duty of every man who assumes to be the head of a family, to procure a comfortable habitation for that family. Some men think too lightly of this, and by unfaithfulness and neglect attempt to rear their families in small uncomfortable and unwholesome abodes, where worriment for the wife, and suffering for the children, continually abound. The limits of this volume prevent dilating on this particular, but a word to the wise is sufficient. Where parents cordially unite in training their children in comfortable homes, we expect children reared who will prove a comfort and honor to their parents and ornaments of society. But where these prerequisites are not found, and children neglected, and in the absence of enjoyment at home left to roam the streets, imbibing vicious principles and contracting evil habits, we expect as a natural consequence they will grow up to be a pest to society and a scourge to their parents. Hence blessed, thrice blessed, are those parents who have trained up their children aright.

We ask the indulgence of the reader for this digression, given for the purpose of showing the opposite effects of the faithful or negligent parent on the subsequent life of the children and on society.

We trace the excellence of the life of Mis-Miller to the enjoyments of her home under the special attention of kind parents, who have never regretted the time, expense and care given to her early culture.

CHAPTER III.

Removal to Chulasky—Benevolent Enterprise of Samuel R. Wood—Every Child of seven years learns to read in Six Months after opening the School—Return to Turbutville—Development of the Public School System—Educational Association of Northern Pennsylvania.

WHEN she was about four years old, her father engaged as teacher and minister at Chulasky Furnace, within three miles of Danville, Pa., established by Samuel R. Wood, who had been included in a constellation of eminent philanthropists of Philadelphia, among whom was Roberts Vaux, Matthew Carey, Alexander Henry, Revs. Drs. Skinner, Brantly, Ely, Abercrombie, the venerable Bishop White, and others, who distinguished that city by their eminent charitable and beneficent enterprises. Mr. Wood erected a first-class anthracite furnace near Danville, at which he employed hands, numbering with their families, one hundred and fifty souls. The object of this enterprise was not merely to make money and show skill in conducting a large business; but to rear the offspring of his work-hands to virtue, usefulness and happiness; lamenting the fact that the children at such establishments had hitherto been neglected and suffered to grow up in ignorance and vice. Hence, he did not only have furnaces, shops, warerooms, store-houses and dwellings erected, but likewise, as most important of all, a church and school-house, supplied with a teacher during the week and preaching on the Sab-bath, without expense to the workmen, and proving to be a strong inducement for virtuous hands to seek employment there. The church was open twice every Sabbath, and the school open all the year, with the exception of two short vacations. Likewise a Sabbath-school with Library, for which Mr. Wood contributed

$50, and the workmen and friends a larger amount.

This was a beneficent experiment, and such an experiment as has seldom been made with equal success; the liberal appropriation of the proprietor furnishing and supporting the school out of his own funds, save a meager appropriation of the School Board.   But this was not considered the best part of the achievement.

Of the one hundred and fifty employees, the   majority   were   foreigners — Welsh, French, Irish, English, Germans or Scotchmen; some of them infidels, some Roman Catholics, a few Lutherans, and a few of them German Reformed, but very few, if any of them, practical Christians.

The moral and intellectual culture of their children having been almost entirely neglected; seldom has there ever been assembled a more uncouth set of children than made their ap-

pearance on the first day of that school. The
entire number of pupils amounted to about
eighty. Those who were not large enough to
drive carts, or perform some such work, had
been allowed to roam at will over hills and
hollows, or, like the wild ducks, to dabble in
the mud along the banks of the Susquehanna.
Thirty of them had never learned the alphabet. The children of the bosses, managers
and clerks were well clad, and courteous in
manners; but the majority wore apparel that
corresponded with the crudeness of their be-
nighted minds. And yet beneath those tat-
tered garbs there were some bright intellects,
susceptible of as much culture and refinement
as those born in palaces and reared in the lap
of luxury. The spirits of such subject to continued neglect, would be doomed to penury
and woe; but, if properly nurtured might become honored, useful and happy; and, it was
for their special benefit that the school-house

and church had been erected, and a system
devised for their instruction.   What a work of
philanthrophy was here to be accomplished!
How was it to be commenced and how to be
pursued?   The old fashioned school-masters
were accustomed to enter with stern looks,
bearing a rod, and to say, "Boys, you *must
behave yourselves or I'll thrash you.*"   But
the teacher in charge by philanthropic experience had found a more excellent way.   His
accustomed demeanor was gentleness and
kindness, which divested the children of terror
or dread, and secured the esteem of the uncouth and hardened; causing such to feel inferior and yield homage to those of better
breeding.

The first lesson taught was cleanliness.   The
children were reminded, that, as it was a new
house with nicely painted desks and seats, that
they should come with clean hands and feet,
and not soil the seats or desks or walls, and

let the teacher make the first scratch any where about the building. Thus, from the beginning they were taught tidiness and purity as the essential foundation of bodily comfort and the best test of true religion. For the Saviour said " Blessed are the pure in heart, for they shall see God."

This was a new and a strange lesson for furnacemen's children. We do not assert it in reproach to all, some were genteelly clad ; others, from their kind of work found it una- voidable to soil their clothing. But we wished to inculcate the idea of clean hands as indica- tive of pure hearts, having no faith in the idea of dirty or sluggish Christians; and it was found to have a salutary influence on the parents as well as on their children. There was soon an improvement in their apparel and in their houses, and all cordially assented to the propriety of the same.

The next statute, or rule, was that each

scholar was to have a particular seat, not to be changed except by the order or consent of the teacher.

The third statute was, no scholar to speak during school hours, except in recitation or when addressing the teacher, or for a special purpose, by permission of the teacher.

The fourth statute was, as order is heaven's first law, therefore, there would be a time and place for everything. A time to come to school; a time for recess; a time to dismiss school; a time for each particular recitation or exercise; for each class, and for each scholar. And these all to be denoted by the teacher on the signal bell.

These few brief rules were easily understood, and easily complied with, by every scholar, and found to be all that was needed for the proper regulation of the school. The teacher arranged the classes and designated the time or each exercise and recitation, so as to keep the attention of all occupied, without detaining them long enough to become weary.

Some may ask how could a school of eighty scholars be conducted without any talking or changing seats? The reply is, give them something to think about, keep them busy, and let the teacher teach them, rather than say to the scholars, " *Go and learn*," when they did not understand the lesson. Thus let the difficult branches be explained and interspersed by the teacher with brief lectures on geography, history, ancient and modern; natural history, botany, etc. If the teacher understands those topics, he will be able to illustrate them with brief, pertinent anecdotes, that will prove interesting and secure the attention and esteem of his scholars. Then he will need no rod, and seldom have occasion to reprove truants, nor to call any to account for absence, or for late attendance ; and the pupils will feel much better when school is dismissed than if they had passed the time without rule and order, having all systematically arranged for one recitation to succeed another without delay, so as to keep all occupied ; one class preparing while another was reciting, some writing on slates, while others were reading, and all moving on methodically, so as to leave no vacant time, except the regular recess for mental relaxation and bodily exercise.

By this means those scholars became so much delighted with the exercises of that school that it was difficult for their mothers to keep them at home to go errands.

The fame of the school spread far around, and those of more opulent circumstances resorted there to learn the rules and to adopt the examples.

It was likewise noticed that, although their mothers were taxed with more attention to their clothing, yet they were amply repaid by more care taken of that clothing, better deportment, and, consequently, more domestic happiness.

But most, and best of all, the scholars made rapid progress in learning. Before the school was in operation six months, every child within reach of that school that was seven years of age could read, including all of the thirty who began in the alphabet.

The school was uniformly opened by reading a chapter of the Bible, and closed by singing an appropriate hymn or ode, observing always to enliven the spirits of the scholars with music and some brief, pleasant address before dismissing them.

The system of instruction having proved successful, showing the practicability of interesting children in the exercises of the school-room, so as to excite a fondness rather than dislike, and to have them become discreet and manly in deportment, and to learn to read correctly before they were seven years old, the proprietor and his friends congratulated themselves that they had accomplished a good work.

As a specially gratifying result, about twenty of these scholars early gave satisfactory evidences of piety, and united, as well as some of their parents, with different branches of the Protestant churches, and one of them, the son of a French Roman Catholic, who was an eloquent declaimer, entered the University at Lewisburg as a candidate for the ministry.

However, an unfavorable change in the iron business occurring, Mr. Wood found it inconvenient to continue his patronage, and, turning the school over to the Public School Board, Mr. M. returned to his previous residence, at Turbutville, in 1852.

While at Chulasky, Henrietta became noted as a good reader, and she likewise became fond of reading the publications of the A. S. S. U. A. T. Society, and other books suitable to her age, as found in the Sunday-school library, or supplied by her parents or friends. She likewise manifested much interest in the exercises of the Sabbath-school and of the church, and showed a special interest in family worship.

Upon returning to Turbutville, she pursued elementary studies under the direction of her mother; and when she was about seven years old, an aunt made her a present of an accordion, and Mrs. Cox, an excellent lady, living in the next house, taught her to play a few tunes on that instrument.

Finding her capable of learning at that early age, others were encouraged, and there was a class of twelve little girls formed, whose parents procured the accordions, and a juvenile band soon beautified their homes and enlivened the village with their delightful music, showing that children are capable of acquiring a knowledge of vocal and instrumental music at a very early age, and nothing more adapted to make a home more happy than music.

There will be no jars, or strife, nor inert minds where the melody of music is found. A home thus supplied will afford the inmates stronger attachments and purer charms than revelry and giddy mirth. Hence, parents had better incur the expense of musical instruments, with competent instructors, than to suffer their children to grow up without.

It may be proper, in this connection, to give a sketch of the development of the public school system of Pennsylvania, and show how singularly the subject of these memoirs was found at the time of acquiring her education to have had her lot amongst those who were conspicuous actors in its development.

This school at Chulasky was a link in a series of educational developments by which the minds of philanthropists expanded into vigorous activity throughout the State, maturing a system of free common schools for the benefit of all classes, for the poor as well as for the rich, and thus bringing them into a proximity they had not known before.

The population increasing rapidly, there was obvious necessity of increasing the number of the schools and improving the arrangements to properly conduct and support them. Hence, in 1830, there was a bill reported in the Legislature of Pennsylvania, to amplify the means of educating the poor; which, prior to that time, had been on a very limited scale.

Simultaneous with this free-school movement a cordial union of the leading Christian denominations, to form humane and benevolent institutions for the purpose of restraining vice and of promoting the blessings of the gospel, was awakened throughout the land. Hence the American Sunday-school Union was formed on the 1st of May, 1825, and that day may with great propriety be esteemed a memorable day, when good men of the leading denominations united their wisdom and with glowing eloquence urged the establishment of this beneficent institution, that the children might be taught *to remember the Sabbath day and keep it holy.* In 1826, such men as the Rev. Drs. Lyman Beecher and Edwards, of Boston, with Beeman, of New York, and other kindred spirits, deploring the torrent of·intemperance, that was hurling multitudes to perdition, raised the alarm that received favorable response from many hearts, and temperance societies formed, and multitudes pledged to neither *touch, taste,* nor *handle* intoxicating liquors.

Then, as better attractions and employment for young men, Libraries, Lyceums and Reading-rooms, with Young Men's Prayer-meetings were established. And as an outgrowth of all this, in 1827, the American Tract Society was formed, with the view of furnishing evangelical religious books in a cheap form, to be scattered broadcast over the land. Thus the leading doctrines of the Holy Scriptures were published in small tracts, and distributed free in the towns, from house to house, and colporteurs sent through the country, thus spreading the light of divine truth amongst all classes of society.

Another coincidence: As a natural result there were about this period numerous revivals of religion, more general and more especially interesting than ever known in this or any other land since the time of the Reformation. Hence it is not surprising to find that amidst the diffusion of so much unvarnished gospel truth, there would be a simultaneous desire for expanding the system of common school instruction. And it is worthy of remark, that the men who were most zealous and useful in forwarding temperance societies, Sabbath schools, and evangelical piety, were those who were the most active in promoting the improvement of our free schools. And those who opposed our free common school system were those who derided revivals, opposed Sunday-schools and tract societies, and were especially hostile to temperance societies, although they were the persons who, with their families, most needed the benefit of them.

These multiplied means adopted, and enlisting the energies of all classes, there was a general desire to mature systems, and aim at perfection in practicing them. Hence for the better development, we find Teachers' Institutes and Normal Schools established. The former, with the view of bringing teachers frequently together in social harmony, to compare their respective methods, that one might derive benefit by comparison with the others; the latter (Normal Schools), where teachers might *teach teachers how to teach*—and as a sequel to these auxiliaries, the idea of County Superintendency; to have a person of suitable qualifications to examine the teachers, and to visit all the schools and see that they were properly conducted. The credit of originating this office, we believe, is due to the Hon. Thos. H. Burrowes, former Secretary of the Commonwealth, who likewise started the *School Journal*, which he ably conducted until it became well established, and was taken under the legislative patronage.

Along with other agencies to enlighten the public mind and to establish the Public School System, there was also organized, in 1853, the Educational Association of Northern Pennsylvania, composed of teachers and other friends of education, with the Rev. Howard Malcomb, D. D., President, Rev. J. W. Barritt and Rev. H. Miller, Vice-Presidents, and Wm. Burgess, Principal of Millville Boarding School, Secretary. This Association met quarterly. Held a meeting at Williamsport, Jersey Shore, Lewisburg and Danville. The object was to mature our Common School System and to promote the cause of education, temperance and true piety by every laudable method.

Each meeting proved to be a real intellectual feast that was much enjoyed by all the members of the Association, and evidently accomplished much good, by preparing the public mind to adopt the county superintendency and make ample legislative appropriations to establish a matured system of Common Schools on a permanent basis.

CHAPTER IV.

Rapid   Intellectual   Development—Proficiency   in
Music—Interest   in   Sabbath-school   and   Religious
Literature—Systematic Bible Reading.

W E now return to the subject of these
memoirs.   Being an only child, and
possessed of superior attractions, she received
all the kind attention that Christian parents
could bestow, and, in return, her amiability
and intelligence endeared her very strongly to
them.   Of her own accord, she devoted a portion of each day to books, and to the study
and practice of music.   She likewise early became delighted with various kinds of fancy
work, to which she devoted a portion of her
leisure hours, beginning with tatting and guard-
chains, knitting tidies of various beautiful pat-
terns, scarfs, nubias, shawls, and gloves; with
different kinds of paintings, including oil and

(47)

water colors; with wax work of fruit and flowers, zephyr work, crotchet work, leather and
shell frames, needle work, with other choice
fancy work, until every room in her residence
was embellished with specimens of her laudable industry, exquisite taste and skill.

Thus, her intellectual faculties were developed, while her time was usefully and credit-
ably employed.

From the amount of knowledge thus acquired, she was capable of interesting her
visitors by a recital of what she had read in
the excellent books provided for her, and in
displaying the numerous articles of her handi-
work, thus making her home especially pleasant at all times.

'As she grew up, she took pleasure in out-
door exercises, and manifested a relish for the
delights that nature affords in a well-arranged
lawn and garden. Hence, her residence was
surrounded with flowers and shrubbery, with

fruit, and ornamental, and shade trees, until upwards of fifty choice varieties were there blooming of her judicious selection.

Thus, she was occupied either in intellectual pursuits, or in some useful manual exercises, with no disposition to loiter or squander time in idleness, nor for gadding or gossip. Nor had she any relish for fictions or novel reading. She often said there is too much useful knowledge to be acquired to waste precious time in reading romance or fiction.

She preferred associates who were intelligent, of discreet behavior, and truly pious. Being sedate, and not disposed to make a vain show, much of her real merit was unknown to those who were not intimately acquainted with her. Being graceful in deportment, and cheerful in disposition, she uniformly secured the esteem of all who knew her.

At the advice of her father, she kept a journal containing the names of the books she had read, with a synopsis of their contents, from which to review and refresh the memory; and thus she laid up a large stock of useful knowledge.

Her first primer, and first spelling-book, and first school readers used by her are all preserved,—almost as sound and as free from blemishes as when they were purchased.

When about seven years old, while living at Turbutville, she became interested in reading the *Child's Paper*, published by the American Tract Society; and taking a specimen copy of it went through the village, procured a club of subscribers for it, and thus introduced and circulated that attractive and useful juvenile publication, which practice she continued annually during her residence at that place.

Her mind thus became imbued with excellent sentiments, inculcated by the books she read as well as by oral instruction. She adopted principles and practices of the purest and most elevated kind, and had very little relish for the company of those children who, having been neglected by their parents, passed their time in idleness or in roaming the streets or fields.

She was early enrolled as a member of the Sabbath-school. She attended regularly from year to year, and preferred being a scholar to study and learn, even after she was considered competent to be a teacher. Her attendance was cheerful, and her lessons regularly studied and well recited, even when a small child.

The instruction she there received proved to be an important help in her religious education. She was early convinced of the importance of religion, and respect was thus excited in her mind for the Bible as the Word of God, and for the Sabbath as the Lord's day, so that she did not trifle with the means of grace as some children who have not had the benefit of early instruction and restraint.

Her behavior in time of religious worship,
even in childhood, was respectful, and in the
Sabbath-school her amiable and good conduct
always procured for her the love of the
teachers.

She esteemed her Sabbath-school teacher of
Turbutville very highly, who was an intelligent
and devoted pious widow lady, who had a
daughter of her own age, with whom she delighted to associate and to remain with over
night to engage with them in their family worship.

She adopted of her own accord a systematic
plan of reading the Bible, and read it entirely
through in regular course from the first of
Genesis to the last of Revelation by the time
she was ten years old. Then repeating, during her eleventh year, she read that precious
book entirely through the second time, and
instead of becoming tired of it, the more she
read the more interest she felt in it, and con-

tinued the practice, so that it is not known that she ever after passed a day without reading more or less in the Bible, except when traveling or when prostrated on a bed of sickness.

Hence her ample knowledge and cheerful hope from that source fully prepared her for a remarkably happy close of life ; and let it encourage the female Christian that many have preceded her who like Ruth, and Hannah, and Mary, and Dorcas, and Priscilla, have been accepted, have finished their work, received their crown of glory, and are now with the spirits of the just made perfect.

Her life from childhood shows the great utility of making home pleasant for children, and awakening a relish for intellectual culture at an early age. Their tender minds and hearts, and likewise their bodily health, will be thus protected, and the Lord will add His blessing on all faithful paternal culture. But if this is neglected, the youthful mind becomes stultified, the faculties blunted, tainted, and depraved. If not developed by wise counsel, and the good examples of pious parents, it will be vitiated by the evil influences of those who fear not God, nor regard their own souls. In the month of March, 1858, Henrietta's father became Principal of the Juniata Academy, in which was employed a teacher of music, and she with other pupils received regular instruction in this her favorite branch of studies. By assiduity in study, with a commendable desire to become proficient, she made a gratifying progress, and acquired in course of time the reputation of being a good musician. There were few to be found who were better versed in this science, and very few who understood it so well. The publishers often sent her specimen sheets of new music, which after examination and a little practice she would play with the greatest accuracy. During a recess in the summer of 1860, it was thought that a change of scenery, with a change of musical instructor, might be grati- fying and beneficial to her. Hence she was placed under the care of Mr. J. B. Meyers, of Aaronsburg, Centrè county, Pa., for several months, who had the reputation of being a superior musician. His residence, known as "Rose Hill," was delightfully situated one mile east of the town, with abundance of ripe peaches and other delicious fruit and rich cream. Mr. Meyers, likewise, had two daugh- ters, who were near Henrietta's age. So that with genial companions and luscious fare the sojourn proved to be a real musical elysium. During her two months' stay, in the height of enjoyment, she made considerable progress in the practice of music, and gained two inches in height.

CHAPTER V.

Removal to Phœnixville—Joins German Reformed Church—Enters Linden Cottage Seminary—Removal to Adamstown—Becomes a Teacher—Removal to Waynesboro—Organist of Trinity Church —Teacher of Fairview School—System of Teaching —Teachers' Institutes.

THE war coming on in the spring of 1861, that, with various other occurrences, induced a removal to Phœnixville, the place of Mr. M.'s nativity. Here Henrietta joined the German Reformed Church, under the pastoral care of the Rev. A. B. Shenkle, and became a teacher in both the Presbyterian and German Reformed Sabbath-schools. The former met in the forenoon, the latter in the afternoon. She became teacher of a class in each, and was punctual and faithful in attendance. She had an especially interesting class of little girls for her morning class, including two daughters of the Rev. Mr. Porter, pastor of the church, who usually likewise attended, and instructed a Bible class.

In 1866 she entered Linden Cottage Seminary for Young Ladies, in the city of Reading, with an arrangement for a regular course of studies, and to render certain specified services as assistant teacher. Hence she escorted the young ladies, pupils of the Seminary, in their morning walks of half an hour through the city every morning before breakfast, and twice on the Sabbath to church; either to Dr. Bausman's or to Dr. McCauley's, where seats were reserved for them. She sat with them during study hour, and was sometimes entrusted with the charge of the Institution during the absence of the Principal from Friday till Monday. By close application to study she made rapid progress, and by exemplary deportment gained much esteem while connected with this Seminary.

In 1867 the family moved to Adamstown, where the school directors tendered Miss M. a position in the borough schools, which she filled with acceptance; and taught a private school in her own house during the intervals of the terms of the public schools. She was organist of the Sabbath-school, and her musical performances were much applauded. How often did throngs gather and persons pause while passing her residence to hear her play on the organ, and sing *"Sweet Hour of Prayer,"* *"In the Christian's Home in Glory,"* *"On the Other Side,"* with other soul-stirring favorite hymns, that she rendered with much effect to the gratification of those who duly appreciated her real piety and musical talents.

Upon moving to Waynesboro, in the autumn of 1872, she was elected organist of the choir and of the Sabbath-school of Trinity Reformed Church, which office she faithfully filled, without recompense and without being absent, except in case of sickness, until within a few days of her death.

She was likewise elected by the school directors as the teacher of Fairview school, which she accepted in preference to two others that were offered with a larger salary.

Here was found an intelligent and liberal-minded Board of Directors, with a modern planned school-house, recently erected on an eminence, appropriately styled Fairview, commanding an extensive prospect of the beautiful Cumberland Valley, and of the distant mountains on either side. It was a neat structure, with improved patented seats and desks, with black surface extending across the building for writing exercises. The directors were liberal in furnishing maps, charts, diagrams, cards, and object-lessons.

Miss M. filled out the paraphernalia by procuring a dozen appropriate mottoes, arranged on the walls, with a choice variety of the portraits of distinguished persons, landscapes, paintings, flowers in hanging baskets, fancy articles, puzzles, and other articles that were instructive, ornamental, and highly entertaining—the sight of which was exhilarating to the scholars, and calculated to enlist their attachment to the place. She was deeply interested in the general subject of education, and gave much attention to the practice of teaching, from her own experience and observation, by a personal acquaintance with prominent educators, and attendance and participation at several popular teachers' institutes —one at Lancaster, where these institutes originated, and were fostered by Professor Wickersham, the Hon. Thomas H. Burrowes, and their coadjutors; one at Phoenixville, conducted by Mr. Maris, county superintendent, assisted by Bayard Taylor, the celebrated traveler, George Francis Train, and others;

another at Reading, with six hundred and fifty
teachers, conducted by Professor Bruner, assisted by Mrs. Logee, Rev. Mr. Willitts, and
other popular lecturers; and for several years
attended the annual meetings of the Franklin
County Teachers' Institute, and participated
in the exercises at Chambersburg. Thus, by
improving favorable opportunities, and cher-
ishing an unselfish desire to become proficient
in her profession, she matured plans of arrang-
ing her school, of governing and imparting
instruction, that proved highly successful.

She considered a favorable location and
proper arrangements of the building, with
suitable furniture, of great importance, so that
all should be attractive and nothing repulsive
to children about the school. She likewise
deemed it important that the school-room
should be kept clean; hence it was swept daily
and scrubbed at least once a month.

Tidiness and cleanliness were considered

important for every school, and an essential basis of probity in after life.

The following brief Code of Rules was suspended for all to see—to wit:

RULES.

Scholars are expected to comply with the following rules:

1st. That they appear in the school-room at the appointed time for commencing, or bring a reasonable excuse.

2d. That they do not, without permission, speak to any one during the session, except to the instructor.

3d. That they do not leave their seats without permission.

Thus, having a house suitably located, and properly furnished, the next in order was to put in operation a judicious system of government and instruction, which of course devolved on the teacher—not on the pupils,

patrons, nor directors—and consisted in car-
rying out the idea of the teacher, teaching
what the pupils were expected to learn. The
former custom of many to give scholars books
and say to them, *"You must go and learn;"*
"You must do this," and *"You must not do
that,"* was discarded. At the appointed time
the signal bell called the school to order; each
one being seated, the teacher at her place read
a portion of the Bible. Her reading, like her
singing, was such that all would distinctly understand, and hence was listened to with close
attention. It was frequently remarked that
very few preachers produced more serious impressions by their pulpit exercises than Miss
Miller did by reading the Scriptures.

The school being thus formally opened, the
next was to proceed with the routine of exercises. This the teacher denoted by the signal
bell; the scholars all knew and understood
the significance of the ring, the tap, or the

rattle, and complied with the various evolutions indicated thereby. The classes thus summoned to the stand were briefly addressed, and each exercise preceded by a few explanatory remarks. Some of the lessons for the primary classes were versified and set to music, and sung at intervals, by way of recreation, and to impress the contents indelibly on the minds of all. Thus the alphabet, the arithmetical tables, the outlines of geography, of ancient and modern history, and of astronomy, were versified and sung, with occasional exercises in calisthenics, in which all delighted, and which proved to be a pleasing interlude to the more monotonous and difficult studies.

But, essential as a well-furnished house with a judicious arrangement of exercises may be, it will be found that the qualifications and deportment of the teacher are of the greatest importance, and it is these that give character and success to a school. There are very few men who are capable of controlling an army, as Generals Washington, Jackson or Grant did; and it is the smallest number of those who engage as teachers who are capable of conducting a school, or who are successful in their sphere.

Those who undertake to teach merely for the sake of the salary, or because they could get no other employment; who, without the intellectual qualifications and without a matured system, would uncouthly enter a school-room and attempt in an arbitrary manner to enforce discipline by a dexterous use of the rod, or by a coaxing and sycophantic dalliance towards their pupils, will be more likely to excite disgust than to secure respect, and much more likely to make truants and knaves than scholars. Miss Miller required no such subterfuges, and she very seldom had any occasion to enforce discipline. Her dignified deportment, mixed with social kindness, secured profound respect, with a cordial compliance with all her rules. There was a continual mutual attachment between her and her pupils, with rare exceptions (of such as had been badly trained at home), and that attachment seemed augmenting, while she was evidently rising in the estimation of the community, with the cheerful prospect of a career of honor and usefulness before her. But, even with the fairest prospects, how true that " *the path of glory leads but to the grave.*"

CHAPTER VI.

Failing Health—Christmas Festival—Last Illness—
Not Afraid to Die—Dying to Live Again—Funeral
Services.

OUR lives are as vapors that appear for a
little time, but soon vanish away. During the month of August preceding her death,
she was prostrated by bilious fever for several
weeks; but regained her health so as to be
able to resume her school in October; and
three weeks prior to her death she attended
the annual meeting of the Franklin County
Teacher's Institute at Chambersburg, in which
she participated, and evidently enjoyed the
exercises very much: returning home appar-
ently with improved health and with cheerful
anticipations. At these Institutes she extended her acquaintance amongst teachers,
popular educators and lecturers; thus add-

ing to her stock of knowledge and maturing plans to become proficient in her profession and extensively useful as a teacher.

The cause of education and of piety lay near her heart, and she seemed fervently desirous to do all in her power to promote them. The choir of which she was organist was preparing for a Christmas Festival. They had made selections; and at a musical rehearsal of some difficult pieces on the night of the 16th of December, she played the organ about two hours in an over-heated room; became fatigued, and returning home through a piercing cold wind with the ground covered with snow, she became chilled; typhoid fever ensued, with which she suffered severely and died in just one week !

What a mystery in the events of Divine Providence, that one in the prime life, so amply qualified to be useful, so much needed and so much esteemed; with a willing heart to employ her talents for the good of society, to be thus taken away from a field of useful labor, and with the most encouraging prospects before her.

But it was the Lord's doing, and we must submit.

> Happy spirit, thou art fled
>> Where no grief can entrance find;
> Lulled to rest the aching head,
>> Soothed the.sorrows of the mind.

During her last illness she suffered severely, and the disease baffled the best medical skill; but she was patient, and like a valiant hero met the king of terrors without dismay. She had such delightful views of the heavenly world that she was thus divested of gloom or dread.

About thirty-six hours before her departure, while in full possession of her mental faculties, perceiving symptoms of dissolution, she called her parents to her bedside, and said to them

that she had had a presentiment for some time
that she would not live to see another Christmas, and from present impressions thought
she would die that night; and lest she would
lose her reason and not know them at the
time, she wished to tell them that *she was not
afraid to die! She had made her peace with
God. Had a hope that cast out fear. Death
had no terrors for her. She was going home
to Heaven, and would be there to welcome them
when they came.* She said, *Tell our Sabbath
school teachers and scholars that I want to
meet them all in heaven; tell them for me, that
if any of them are not prepared,* TO PREPARE *and
not put it off another day!* Seeming solicitous,
she appealed to her father and asked him if
he would tell them? and upon receiving his
promise that he would do so, she continued
saying, *Tell them to remember me when they
sing those beautiful hymns that I used to play
for them on the organ, especially when they*

sing the last verse of the last hymn we sung the last time I was in the church. * Tell my Fairview scholars that I said, they should all be good boys and girls and prepare to meet me in Heaven.* Then added, *I loved those scholars, and was anxious to do them all the good I possibly could.* Continuing said, *she had always been fond of music and was now going to join the heavenly choir. We will have harps of gold and superior music to that of earth. There will be no discord there; but all will be harmony and love.* She continued speaking thus for near an hour in a train of the most elevated heavenly sentiments—interspersed by singing parts of several appropriate hymns—

O think of the home over there,
By the side of the river of light,
Where the saints all immortal and fair,
Are robed in their garments of white.
Over there—over there,
Oh think of the home over there.

---

* Found in the Appendix. *The Good Old Way.*

After some other remarks, she sang a part of
the hymn beginning with

In the Christian's home in glory there remains a rest
for me.

And again after other remarks she sang a part
of the hymn beginning

Shall we meet in heaven ?

But it would be impossible to convey a true
idea of the solemn manner of her utterance.
Pausing for a few moments, she then made a
verbal distribution of her property ; and particularly presented a Bible to her mother that
she had purchased in Chambersburg during
the meeting of the Teacher's Institute only
about two weeks before ; and on doing so
with special emphasis said : MA, READ IN
THAT BIBLE EVERY DAY !

Finally looking upward, she said, *she saw
the pearly gates of Heaven standing open, and
a throng of Angels, robed in white, beckoning
her home.*

Continuing to gaze she said : THEY ARE COMING TO MEET ME ! *They are almost here! There is but a little cloud between us, and I must go!* Then extending her hand first to her father and then to her mother she said, GOOD-BYE PA ! GOOD-BYE MA! (shaking hands with each of them) and added : I AM GOING TO DIE TO LIVE AGAIN ! and THAT WILL BE A DEATH WORTH LIVING FOR ! Having thus spoken, she gradually relapsed into calm repose, without speaking any more except in brief responses, until her gentle spirit in the most serene manner took its departure to the glorified mansions of the blest. Seldom have the sentiments of the following anthem, known as the Dying Christian, been so literally exemplified as in the dying scenes of Miss Miller.

> Vital spark of heavenly flame,
> Quit, oh quit, this mortal frame ;
> Trembling, hoping, lingering, flying,

4

Oh! the pain the bliss of dying.
Cease, fond nature, cease thy strife,
And let me languish into life:
Hark!   They whisper; Angels say,
Sister spirit come away;
What is this absorbs me quite?
Steals my senses, shuts my sight,
Drowns my spirits, draws my breath,
Tell me, my soul, can this be death?
The world recedes, it disappears,
Heaven opens on my eyes, my ears
With sounds seraphic ring;
Lend, lend your wings, I mount, I fly.
Oh grave! where is thy victory,
Oh death! where is thy sting?

Her unexpected death produced a deep impression on the entire community; not merely
on her parents who were thus bereft of an
only child, who had been a solace to them in
old age; and on account of her superior excellence had become much endeared to them.
But all appeared to feel her loss.   Just one

week before her death she was in apparent
good health performing her part on the organ •
with peculiar grace at a musical rehearsal;
leading those rich tones of delightful music
and awakening a rapturous anticipation of the
approaching Christmas festival. But now her
graceful form is missed and her voice no more
heard upon the earth.

She has ascended to the glorified mansions
and is now associated with an innumerable
multitude of saints and of the spirits of the
just made perfect around the throne of God,
engaged in the exercises of the upper sanc-
tuary.

Her funeral was numerously attended by
those of the different denominations, by
teachers of the public schools, by Sabbath-
school teachers and teachers of music. The
Sabbath-school of Trinity Reformed church,
numbering about two hundred, in which she
was a teacher, attended in procession from

her late residence. The casket containing her remains was conveyed into the church and placed before the altar. While entering the church an appropriate solemn dirge was performed that added to the solemnity of the scene. The Rev. Mr. Hibshman, pastor of the church, preached an impressive and appropriate sermon, assisted in the service by the Rev. Mr. Kesler, after which the interment was made, near on the right of the entrance to the church.

"OVER THERE."

[Sung by Miss Miller in her dying moments.]

1. *Oh ! think of the home over there,*
   By the side of the river of light,
   Where the saints all immortal and fair,
   Are robed in the garments of white.

   Refrain—Over there, over there,
   Oh, think of the home over there.

2. Oh, think of the friends over there,
   Who before us the journey have trod,

Of the songs that they breathe on the air,
In their home in the palace of God.

Over there, over there,
Oh, think of the friends over there.

3. My Saviour is now over there,
There my kindred and friends are at rest;
Then away from earth's sorrow and care,
Let me fly to the land of the blest.

Over there, over there,
My Saviour is now over there.

4. I'll soon be at home over there,
For the end of my journey I see;
Many dear to my heart over there,
Are watching and waiting for me.

Over there, over there,
I'll soon be at home over there.

I KNOW THOU HAST GONE.

[Written on the death of a dear friend.]

I know thou hast gone to the home of thy rest—
Then why should my soul be so sad?
I know thou hast gone where the weary are blest,

And the mourner looks up and is glad!
Where love has put off, in the land of its birth,
　The stains it had gather'd in this,
And Hope, the sweet singer that gladden'd the earth,
　Lies asleep on the bosom of Bliss.

I know thou hast gone where thy forehead is starr'd
　With the beauty that dwelt in thy soul;
Where the light of thy loveliness cannot be marr'd
　Nor thy heart be flung back from its goal;
I know thou hast drunk of the Lethe, that flows
　Through a land where they do not forget,
That sheds over memory only repose,
　And takes from it only regret!

In thy far away dwelling, wherever it be,
　I believe thou hast visions of mine,
And the love that made all things a music to me,
　I yet have not learnt to resign.
In the hush of the night, in the waste of the sea,
　Or alone with the breeze on the hill,
I have ever a presence that whispers of thee,
　And my spirit lies down and is still!

Mine eye must be dark, that so long has been dimm'd,
　Ere again it may gaze upon thine;

But my heart has revealings of thee and thy home,
  In many a token and sign!
I never look up, with a vow, to the sky,
  But a light like thy beauty is there,
And I hear a low murmur, like thine, in reply,
  When I pour out my spirit in prayer.

And though like a mourner that sits by a tomb
  I am wrapp'd in a mantle of care,
Yet the grief of my bosom—oh! call it not gloom—
  Is not the black grief of despair.
By sorrow reveal'd as the stars are by night,
  Far off a bright vision appears:
And hope, like the rainbow, a creature of light,
  Is born, like the rainbow, from tears.

THE GOOD OLD WAY.

This was the last piece practiced by the choir
at rehearsal, and the last time Miss Miller performed her part as organist, just one week
before her death:

  We are going forth with our staff in hand
  Thro' a desert wild in a stranger land;

But our faith is bright and our hope is strong
And the good old way is our pilgrim song.

CHORUS—

'Tis the Good Old Way that our fathers trod;
'Tis the way of life that leadeth unto God,
'Tis the only path to the realms of day
We are going home in the Good Old Way.

There are foes without, and foes within,
Who would turn us back to the ways of sin;
But we'll stop our ears to the words they say,
While we onward press in the Good Old Way.

In the blissful hour of communion sweet
We will come with joy to the mercy seat;
For we love to sing and we love to pray
And we bless the Lord for the Good Old Way.

On the brink of time when we stand at last,
When our sun has set and our work is past;
When we bid farewell to our mortal clay,
We will praise the Lord for the *Good Old Way.*

CHAPTER VII.

Tributes to Her Memory—Resolution of Teachers' Institute—Letters of Condolence—Death of Two of Her Friends—Dying Words of Pious Women—Love for the Dead—Early Intellectual Development the Result of Parental Care.

THE next day after her death an affectionate memorial appeared in the columns of the *Village Record*, published in the village. The next issue contained tributes of respect to her memory adopted in a series of resolutions by the Sabbath-school Association to which she had been organist and teacher; and similar resolutions by the School Board, by whom she had been employed as a teacher of Fairview school.

The Adamstown *Press*, in alluding to her death, termed her an "estimable young lady." The Lancaster *Express* represented her as "an accomplished teacher;" the *Indepen-*

dent Phœnix, of "*superior rank;*" the *School Journal* and *Christian World* each published eulogistic notices.   But the most definite expression of respect for her memory was given by the Franklin County Teachers' Institute, at their annual meeting held in Chambersburg, one year after her death, which commenced December 1st, and closed Friday, December 5th, 1875, with 260 teachers in attendance.   Mr. W. A. Reed offered the following resolution, which was adopted unanimously :

Resolved, That in the death of Miss Henrietta B. Miller, of Waynesboro, we have lost a faithful teacher, one thoroughly imbued with the love of her profession; graceful in conduct, an exemplary Christian, one beloved in her home and by her scholars, whose memory will not soon be forgotten.

The following obituary article appeared in the April number, 1875, of the Pennsylvania *School Journal*, written by Mr. J. S. Smith, County Superintendent of Franklin co., Pa.;

Henrietta B. Miller, daughter of the Rev. Henry Miller, departed this life at the residence of her father, in Waynesboro, Franklin county, December 23d. She had made teaching a profession. She was a devoted teacher, ever vigilant in the important work of her profession. The steady progress of her school from time to time, is the best evidence of the blessings which crowned her labors. The Christian example which she set before her pupils will, no doubt, prove a blessing to many, leading them to Christ in the morning of their lives. Although she is called from her labors she has gone to enjoy a rich reward.

This mysterious visitation of Providence bears heavily upon her aged parents, who in their sore affliction have the sympathy of the entire community.

J. S. S.

The parents likewise received numerous letters of condolence from personal friends; from clergymen and from prominent friends of education, all showing the high esteem in which she was held, and lamenting the loss of one who bid fair (had her life been spared) for eminent usefulness.

But who would live alway—away from our God,
Away from yon heaven, that blissful abode,
Where the saints of all ages in harmony meet,
Their Saviour and brethren transported to greet,
While the anthems of rapture unceasingly roll,
And the smile of the Lord is the feast of the soul!

The peculiar circumstances of her death forcibly reminded her parents of similar unexpected departures of two of her intimate friends who were about the same age and whose last illness was brought on by exposure to night air. We need not hesitate to mention the name of Sallie Jones, who united with the church at the same time that Henrietta did. They cherished a mutual attachment, attended the same Sabbath-school and exchanged friendly calls. At the anniversary of their Sabbath-school, held in the German Reformed church of Phœnixville, on the night of January 1st, 1863, Sallie and Henrietta stood side by side on the platform and sung an appropriate anthem, enjoying the occasion with genuine youthful ardor, and received the plaudits of the audience. The house was crowded and uncomfortably warm; but the weather was cold and the ground covered with snow, and Sallie having a mile to go to her home, took a cold that resulted in fever with which she suffered several weeks and died. Henrietta repeatedly visited her during her illness, and usually said on her return that "it is better to go to the house of mourning than to the house of feasting." She had ardent affection for her young friend, whom she considered resigned to the will of her blessed Saviour and fully prepared for the heavenly world. She died very happy. The whole community was much affected by her departure. The funeral was numerously attended; for all seemed to realize that a saint had gone to glory.

But how different the end of the third, who had been allured by worldly pleasures from the house of God; and attended what was styled a moon-light hop; where she danced on a platform in the open air until fatigued, and returning home, became the victim of disease that proved fatal. When neither the blandishments of wealth nor the fascinations of worldly pleasure, with all human aid, could propitiate the king of terrors: How different her dying scenes from those of her two former intimate friends! When she found her end was nigh, without a fitness for heaven; what horror filled her heart! In the bitterness of grief she exclaimed "*I am lost!*" And thus the gay and accomplished young lady expired!

As a generous tribute of parental affection, an expensive monument was placed on her grave; which reminds us of her graceful form and elegant attire, but likewise reminds us of her remorse and agonizing death! *Millions of money for an inch of time*, was the doleful

exclamation of Queen Elizabeth in her dying
moments. Multitudes of costly dresses in her
wardrobe, a kingdom at her feet, yet willing
to give millions of money for *an inch of time!*

> Such is the sad uncertainty
> Of sinners here below,
> To-day they float in buoyancy,
> To-morrow drowned in woe!

We here give as appropriate in this connection the

DYING WORDS OF PIOUS WOMEN.

Dying testimonies of rare beauty have fallen
from the lips of pious women, and if less familiar than those of eminent reformers and
divines, they are not less worthy as witnesses
of the power of religion to impart comfort and
triumph at the hour of dissolution. Pious
women as well as worthy men have, when
nearing the heavenly portal, been filled with
exultation and triumph—have seen transporting

prospects from the Delectable Mountains, and
have heard the music of celestial harps and the
ringing of celestial bells.   They have walked
in Beulah, leaning on the arm of their beloved,
and their souls, amid the wrecks of mortality,
have been freshened and exhilarated by the
fragrance and glory of a heavenly atmosphere.
" Oh, those rays of glory !" said Mrs. Clark-
son, when dying,   " My God, I come flying
to thee !" said Lady Alice Lucy.   Lady Hast-
ings said : " Oh, the greatness of the glory
that is revealed to me !"

Beautiful the expression of the dying poet-
ess, Mrs. Hemans :   "I feel as if I were sit-
ting with Mary at the feet of my Redeemer,
hearing the music of his voice, and learning of
him to be meek and lowly."   No poetry, she
said, could express, nor imagination conceive,
the visions of blessedness that flitted across her
fancy, and made her waking hours more delightful than those even that were given to

temporary repose. Similar was the experience of Mrs. Rowe. She said, with tears of joy, that she knew not she had ever felt such happiness in all her life. Hannah More's last words were, " Welcome Joy."

" Oh, sweet, sweet dying !" said Mrs. Talbot, of Reading. " If this be dying," said Lady Glenorchy, "it is the pleasantest thing imaginable." "Victory, victory through the blood of the Lamb !" said Grace Bennet, one of the early Methodists. " I shall go to my Father this night," said Lady Huntington. The dying injunction of the mother of Wesley was, " Children, when I am gone, sing a song of praise to God !"

Looks as well as words often express dying triumph. Says one, after quoting the last prayer of the Countess of Seafield, " With these words she closed her eyes, and seemed to all present to be yielding up her last breath. But in a little time she opened her eyes again, and with an air, as it seemed, of joy and wonder, she continued looking upward with a fixed gaze for nearly half an hour. By degrees she let her eyes fall, shut them, and yielded up her last breath. Those who were present were not a little affected, both with her last words and last looks."

Said Lady Margaret Stewart, forewarning her speedy dissolution, "Sirs, I tell you that this night, when your sun goes down, my sun will arise, and never go down!" She testified, "I have many times besought the Lord that death might be no surprise to me; neither is it. And I have sought that I might not be terrible to others in dying." The sun sank low in the west, and its last rays lit up the hill-tops; she sank to rest amid holy ejaculations and in great elevation of soul.

LOVE FOR THE DEAD.

The love that survives the tomb, says Irving, is the noblest attribute of the soul. If it has woes, it has likewise its delights; and when the overwhelming burst of grief is lulled in the gentle tear of recollection, then the sudden anguish and convulsive agony over the present ruins of all we most loved, are softened away into pensive meditations of all that it was in the days of its loveliness. Who would root such sorrow from the heart; though it may sometimes throw a passing cloud over the bright eyes of gayety, or spread a deeper sadness over the hours of gloom, yet who would exchange it for the song of pleasure or the burst of revelry! No! There is a voice from the tomb sweeter than song; there is a remembrance of the dead, to which we turn even from the charm of the living.

—While reviewing the life of this estimable young person, we find that she imbibed a relish for intellectual culture when quite young, and applied with assiduity to the study of every branch prescribed by her instructors. She was not satisfied with merely sketching ; but aimed at proficiency in every department of study; and hence became expert in solving difficult questions in arithmetic, algebra, geometry, astronomy, history and Latin, and did not considered her studies finished when she left the Seminary ; but continued literary and scientific pursuits *systematically* along with the study and practice of music ; and for relaxation gave some time to painting, in oil and water colors ; with a great variety of fancy work. It may be said she never passed an idle hour—when intellectual exercises were laid aside she found delight in domestic employment, either in the house in the garden, lawn or arbors. More than fifty varieties of fragrant flowers with shade and ornamental trees adorned the surroundings of her dwelling, with various grapes, fruit and the choicest berries of her own selection and culture. The perception of the beauties of nature elevate the affections by inspiring noble reflections that exhilarate the mind and are beneficial to bodily health; while a. home thus decorated and beautified will have much stronger attachments on that account.

She thus early laid the foundation of a liberal education and of an honorable and useful life. The biographers of the celebrated Dr. Doddridge and of the Rev. J. Y. McGennis, state that they both learned to read when only four years old; and it is a remarkable concidence that Miss Miller likewise commenced reading at the same early period, and when only five years astonished the most competent judges including the Rev. Dr. Yeomans, Prof. Robison and Samuel R. Wood, of Danville, by the accuracy of her reading.

The citation of these several instances shows
that hers was not a solitary case, not a prodigy,
but a common result of early faithful parental
attention.   " Just   as   the   twig   is   bent   the
tree   inclines."   If the tender mind and body
of a child is properly nourished, both will
thrive ; if neglected, will famish, or become
dwarfed and effete.

The Hon. J. P. Wickersham, State Superintendent of the common schools of Pennsylvania is credited for stating that the most
important part of education is imparted to
children before they are five years old.

At a Christmas festival of the Sabbath-
school of Trinity Reformed church, Miss M.
prepared a class of three boys and three girls to
sing " *Your Mission*," which was applauded
as a superior performance.   On a similar occasion she prepared two young ladies to sing
with appropriate gestures " *The Christmas
Tree.*"   Having a tree in front of the pulpit,

and the building otherwise decorated, with a crowded audience. The peculiar rendering was very impressive. And on another festival occasion, Miss Vanleer, one of her pupils, sung the solo, "*Beyond the Dark Sea*," which interested the audience very much. Some said "*What a smart child.*" Others remarked, "The young lady must have had a competent teacher, to have taught her to perform with so much excellence."

We give a few extracts from her pen as specimens of her style, and indicating a vigorous intellect, amply stored with useful knowledge.

The first was an *impromptu* sentence given at a teachers' examination held in Washington township. Being asked by the County Superintendent for a specimen of her penmanship, she picked up a pen, and wrote, *May this township, by the intelligence and patriotism of its inhabitants, ever prove worthy of the name it bears.*   H. B. M.

The specimen secured her an award of the highest number, with a plaudit for the sentiment.

While a pupil of Linden Cottage Seminary, she closed a composition with the following noble Christian sentiment:

Sooner cut off a right hand, or pluck out a right eye, than tamely crouch to meanness or vice for the pitiful reward of pleasing those with whom you live, or with whom you are associated, at the expense of making shipwreck of faith and of a good conscience.

In another similar original essay while a pupil of that seminary, she gave an interesting description of the Sacred Mountains referred to in the Bible, with practical remarks, and closed with the following declaration:

The situation and description of each of the Sacred Mountains should be known and remembered by every one who has had the opportunity of learning to read; to be ignorant of such matters is not allowable in these times.

We have before given a description of her school-room, and sketched her method of conducting her school. It may be stated that her motto was *Nil sine labore*, or nothing accomplished without labor. But frequently, when she found a scholar baffled by a hard sum or difficult question, she would with a cheerful air say, *We need* no such word as fail, and give a few suggestions of the rule by way of a start, and then add, " Now try, try and try again." The countenance of the scholar would brighten up, and pursuing her suggestions, soon with an air of triumph he would exclaim, "I have it." Her manner was so affable that she seldom failed to secure the esteem of her pupils. Some of them continue to speak of her in terms of great respect, and often shed tears of affection at the mention of her name.

CHAPTER VIII.

Training of Children—Study of Languages—Value
of Elementary Instruction—Growth of the Scholastic Profession—Rewards of the Faithful Teacher.

IF properly cultivated, children will become
wise and virtuous ; if left shrouded in ignorance, under pernicious influences, the child
may become a ninny and a nuisance, a grief
to its parents and a burden to society. Having
become a good reader and fond of reading,
Miss M. likewise became fond of committing to
memory favorite hymns, poetry, and portions
of Scripture, which gave her a facility in
making quotations, as well as training and
strengthening the mind.

The plea in our colleges for the study of the ·
dead languages is not so much for the sake of
the knowledge thus acquired as for the discipline of the mind. And while it must be con-
ceded that the object would be equally attain-

able by studying our own vernacular tongue, the sentiments of Milton, Cowper, Watts, and other of our English poets, are decidedly preferable to those of Virgil, Ovid, Homer, or Dryden.

To read well is a most useful and agreeable qualification. Yet, important as it is, very few attain that degree of proficiency in it that is attainable; partly owing to injudicious tuition in early life, but chiefly from negligence in mature years.

To read is simply to speak or to repeat the words of another; therefore it is necessary to understand what is read, in order to read it well. First imbibe the sentiment, and then in the most natural manner tell it plainly.

The ample qualifications of Miss M. gave her a controlling influence in the school-room, hall, or social circle. But her generosity exceeded her physical capacity. The combined duties of her school during the week, the choirs

of the church and Sabbath-school three times
on the Sabbath, with her literary labors, show
how her time was incessantly occupied, and
thus she fell a victim to her own beneficence.

These incidents of her life are published in
hopes that by the divine blessing others who
read may be encouraged, and profit by her
worthy example.

In proportion, then, to the immensity of
the power with which we are entrusted, as
guardians of the young, should be the energy
of our exertions to secure them their rich
inheritance—an inheritance of which our own
negligence only can deprive them. By the
power which we may wield through elementary
schools—a power silent, and almost imperceptible in its operations, but sure in its results
—the rising members of our country may be
rendered intelligent, useful, and happy. How
important, then, that the whole energy of this
power be directed to the benefit of the young,

that their expanding intellects receive the perfect aid of early and generous protection and
culture.

As exerting this happy and this powerful
influence upon the interests of society, we
regard all attempts in elementary instruction
as worthy of a hallowed and sublime sympathy.
Their moral power and moral grandeur elevate
our conceptions, and we return to the realities
around us, but to be told how much, very
much, is to be done before the young of our
beloved country can universally enjoy the
rich blessings to which they are entitled. We
regard those who in this department of instruction are successful as the most efficient bene-
factors of mankind. This is indeed a noble
sphere for moralizing the world ; in the grada-
tions of human influence such individuals are
eminently favored. Commencing education
with the very dawn of infant existence, they
may, entertain the pleasing hope of accom-

panying their charge in their juvenile progress, and conducting them to places of honor and usefulness.

With sentiments like these, we are pleased to find instructors commencing their labors in the important department of instruction. We rejoice to see this hitherto much neglected sphere of good—this springtime of life, claiming a degree of attention in some measure proportionate to its immense importance; and we hope the public attention may become still more generally awake to its claims.

The period of childhood and youth is one of beauty, interest and significance; and the subject pertaining to the intellectual and moral culture of children and youth is of primal importance to the State and the Church, as well as to the well-being and eternal destiny of souls.

There are over ten millions of boys and girls in our country between the ages of six

and sixteen. Not much over one-half of this
number attend school. Of the four or five
millions of the colored population, only about
180,500 attend school. Five and a half millions of our people cannot read and write, and
four and a half millions cannot read !

Twenty-five years hence these ten or eleven
millions of boys and girls will be the fathers
and mothers of our country, and some of them
the rulers of the land. Then, in order to
train them for the duties and responsibilities
of life, and to secure them on the side of truth
and righteousness, we must begin NOW. And
how much of this work shall devolve on us?
This is an important and practical question,
and one that demands earnest consideration.

Before closing these memoirs, we wish to
add something for the encouragement of
teachers. Hitherto the inducements have
been comparatively inferior for persons of
either sex to relinquish other avocations and

devote their time and talents to this particular calling. But prospects are brightening. The theory of Teaching has been reduced to a science, as well as that of Law, Medicine and Theology. The scholastic profession now ranks with the most honored and eligible avocations of life. By the accumulation of funds, we have liberal Legislative appropriations. We have in Pennsylvania ten State Normal Schools in which to teach teachers how to teach. With Teachers Institutes in almost every county; with twenty thousand teachers in our common schools, the system has been matured, and the cause of education has been rising so that, according to an opinion recently expressed by Gen. Grant, if there should another national contest arise, we may not expect Mason and Dixon's to be the division line—but ignorance and vice to be on one side, and virtue and intelligence on the other. Good teachers can now get good situations without diffi-

culty. By reference to the annual report of our
State Superintendent for 1875, there were one
hundred and twenty-eight teachers employed in
the city of Reading; five male and one hundred
and twenty-three female, showing that female
teachers are generally preferred. The case of
Mr. John Beck, late principal of the Litiz
Boarding School, shows how that a person of
suitable qualifications, with a mind and heart
for the work, may be successful, honored and
useful. He was a mechanic, became a favorite
of the youth of the place, who expressed a
wish for him to become their teacher and
prevailed upon him to teach a few months ;
but when he intimated an intention to resume
his former vocation, he was beset by a petition signed by every man and woman of the
town to continue. This was irresistible. He
gave himself entirely to the work, and hence,
the popular Boarding School of Litiz, of
which he was Principal for half a century,

during which time he had under his instruction 1896 scholars. These were nearly all from a distance, without advertising or personal effort; and at the time of his death, of the seventy students in attendance, all had come through the influence of former students. Thus did he, and, so may others, pass a happy life in usefulness; and generations yet unborn may enjoy and bless the result of their labors, while at the close of life it will be looked back upon with satisfaction, and the profession of the true teacher esteemed as one of the most creditable among mankind.

Along with Mr. Beck's, we might mention the names of Wm. Rogers, Benjamin Moore, Joshua Hoopes, Edward Foulke, John Comly and Solomon Gause, who were pioneer and patriarchal teachers in the eastern counties of Pennsylvania for many years, who shone as lights in their day, and whose names have been handed down to their posterity with v neration, on account of the hallowed impression they left on society as faithful instructors of the youth.

We may especially refer with peculiar interest to an assemblage of about one hundred and fifty of the former pupils of Solomon Gause who returned to do him homage when his head was silvered o'er with age, on the seventieth anniversary of his birthday. When time had scattered his scholars far and wide in all directions, most of whom were established in various business pursuits for which they had been qualified by the education received in his school, the hallowed recollection of their faithful teacher (their good old friend) induced them to return once more with friendly greetings, bearing testimony of the benefits they had derived from his faithful literary, scientific and moral instruction. They came from the surrounding vicinage, from the adjoining counties, and from distant states—including

those of different ranks, from the humble cob-
bler to the persevering farmer, the energetic
mechanic, the opulent merchant, the eloquent statesman, all having derived profit from
his instruction, and now bringing back tokens
of gratitude for his fidelity as the teacher and
guide of their youth.

Such reward awaits the faithful teacher.
The vocation has its perplexities and its toils.
The waywardness of youth and the ingrati-
tude of parents is disheartening, but instruction given "is like bread cast upon the waters
that is seen after many days." And who
knows but that instruction given to the hum-
blest orphan may rear a patriot, a philanthro-
pist or a herald of the cross, whose fervid
eloquence may resound over the whole earth,
and prove a benefactor to unborn millions
when our bodies are mouldering in the dust.

W E make the following extracts as appropriate advice to those to whom this volume has been dedicated.

PATERNAL CARE.

It is, of course, the first care of religious parents to prepare their children for their eternal state; but it is by fitting them to fill their relations here, that they will best educate them for immortality. Besides the mere communication of religious truth, of what importance is it to regulate the temper, and to direct the mind! How many pious persons have cause to regret their own inconsistencies; the consequence, perhaps, of irritability contracted in childhood, which in maturer years it is very difficult to correct! How often have they to lament their own inertness, the natural effect of early indulgence, which wastes and deadens the intellectual

faculties, and disqualifies them for future
effort ! And though they may struggle against
such evils, and by Divine Grace may be able
to overcome them, they always find that bad
habits are their worst enemies, and that it is
much more easy to discern than to correct
them.

Amiability, intelligence, and an absence of
affectation, are the most delightful features in
female character; and those which next to
religious principle, it is the business of education to impart. And if we would wish our
children to be loved as well as admired, and
esteemed as well as loved ; if we would render
them happy here, fortify them against the
changes of life, and fit them for its close, we
must endeavor to engraft these qualities upon
the solid basis of Christian truth. Religious
parents will, of course, always look to a higher
influence, and will feel the inadequacy of all
human effort ; but they will nevertheless dili-

gently sow the seed, in humble hope; or rather, in full assurance that it will be watered from above.

ON THE STUDIES SUITABLE FOR YOUNG LADIES.

Every woman should consider herself as sustaining the general character of a rational being, as well as the more confined one belonging to the female sex ; and therefore the motives for acquiring general knowledge and cultivating the taste are nearly the same to both sexes. The line of separation between the studies of a young man and a young woman appears to me to be chiefly fixed by this,—that a woman is excused from all professional knowledge. Professional knowledge means all that is necessary to fit a man for a peculiar profession or business. Thus men study in order to qualify themselves for the law, for physic, for various departments in political life, for instructing others from the pulpit or the professor's chair. These all require a great deal of severe study and technical knowledge; much of which is nowise valuable in itself, but as a means to that particular profession. Now as a woman can never be called to any of these professions, it is evident she has nothing to do with such studies. A woman is not expected to understand the mysteries of politics, because she is not called to govern; she is not required to know anatomy, because she is not to perform surgical operations; she need not embarrass herself with theological disputes, because she will neither be called upon to make nor to explain creeds.

HISTORY.

History is among the most agreeable and instructive exercises to which young ladies can apply in order to perfect themselves in the use of languages. It at once gives them an acquaintance with characters and events, and a familiarity with words. It not only gratifies that love of the heroic and the grand, which is inherent in our nature, but also, by setting before us what has happened in the world, prepares us to comprehend and bear whatever may happen to ourselves.

The school discipline of young ladies precludes them from the boisterous exercises which form the principal amusement of youth of the other sex; and the very different and more sedentary mode in which they are trained to fulfill their future station and duties in society, begets in them a greater love of reading than is common to young gentlemen.

There cannot, consequently, be a more important branch of female education, than that which forms their judgment as to the sort of reading upon which their hours of relaxation may be occupied.

It too often happens that the desire, whether

natural or acquired, which most young ladies
have for reading, is so far from being con-
verted into the extremely beneficial instrument of good, which it might be, that in fact
it becomes a cloak for vacuity of mind, and a
source of insignificance and ignorance, which,
once rooted, nothing can uproot. History, abounding with stupendous achievements and astonishing vicissitudes, and every
way calculated to divert as well as instruct
youth, is too frequently read only as a forced
and therefore unpleasant task ; and the leisure
hours, which *History ought* delightfully as well
as profitably to occupy, are worse than wasted,
upon the frivolous or baneful rubbish of the
circulating library. We do not assert that *all*
the contents of a circulating library are either
useless or mischievous: the labors of Scott,
Croly, and Horace Smith, are full of instruction as well as of amusement. But no works
of fiction can be at all comparable to authen-

tic history ; and the generality of those which fill the shelves of the circulating library are calculated, by their unnatural incidents and characters, and their wild and utterly impossible events, to fill the minds of their readers with ridiculous notions, to disgust them with real life, and to pave the way to innumerable and terrible errors.

Our young friends may safely rely upon our correctness in assuring them, that, if they will read history as an amusement, and not as an irksome and imposed task, they will, in tracing the events which it details, the causes and results of those events and the characters connected with them, not merely stock their minds with the most valuable species of human knowledge, but derive from the perusal of every volume of history more exquisite pleasure, than from reading a cart-load of ill-told and ridiculous fictions.

THE USES OF HISTORY.

Much has been said of the uses of history. They are no doubt many, yet do not apply equally to all: but it is quite sufficient to make it a study worth our pains and time, that it satisfies the desire which naturally arises in every intelligent mind to know the transactions of the country, of the globe in which he lives. Facts, as facts, interest our curiosity, and engage our attention.

Suppose a person placed in a part of the country where he was a total stranger; he would naturally ask, who are the chief people of the place, what family they are of, whether any of their ancestors have been famous, and for what. If he see a ruined abbey, he will inquire what the building was used for; and if he be told it is a place where people got up at midnight to sing psalms, and scourged themselves in the day,—he will ask how there came to be such people, or why there are

none now. If he observes a dilapidated
castle which appears to have been battered by
violence, he will ask in what quarrel it suffered, and why they built formerly structures
so different from any we see now. If any
part of the inhabitants should speak a different language from the rest, or have some singular customs among them, he would suppose
they came originally from some remote part
of the country, and would inform himself, if
he could, of the cause of their peculiarities.

If he were of a curious temper, he would
not rest till he had informed himself whom
every estate in the parish belonged to; what
hands they had gone through; how one man
got this field by marrying an heiress, and the
other lost that meadow by a ruinous law-suit.
As a man of spirit he would feel delighted on
hearing the relation of the opposition made
by an honest yeoman to an overbearing rich
man on the subject of an accustomed path-

way or right of common. If he should find
the town or village divided into parties, he
would take some pains to trace the original
cause of their dissension, and to find out, if
possible, who had the right on his side. Circumstances would often occur to excite his
attention. If he saw a bridge, he would ask
when and by whom it was built. If in dig-
ging in his garden he should find utensils of a
singular form and construction, or a pot of
money with a stamp and legend quite different from the common coin, he would be led
to inquire when they were in use, and to whom
they had belonged. His curiosity would ex-
tend itself by degrees. If a brook ran
through the meadows, he would be pleased to
trace it swelled into a river, and the river till
it lost istelf in the sea. He would be asking
whose seat he saw upon the edge of a distant
forest, and what sort of country lay behind
the range of hills that bounded his utmost

view. If any strangers came to visit or reside in the place where he lived, he would be questioning them about the country they came from, their connections and alliances, and the remarkable transactions that had taken place within their memory or that of their parents. The answers to these questions would insensibly grow up into *History*, which, as you see, does not originate in abstruse speculations, but grows naturally out of our situation and relative connections It gratifies a curiosity which all feel in some degree, but which spreads and enlarges itself with the cultivation of our powers, till at length it embraces the whole globe which we inhabit. To know is as natural to the mind as to see is to the eye, and knowledge is itself an ultimate end. But though this may be esteemed an ultimate and sufficient end, the study of history is important to various purposes. Few pursuits tend more to enlarge the mind. It gives us, and it only can give us, an extended knowledge of human nature ;—not human nature as it exists in one age or climate or particular spot of earth, but human nature under all the various circumstances by which it can be affected. It shows us what is radical and what is adventitious; it shows us that man is still man in Turkey and in Lapland, as a vassal in Russia, or a member of a wandering tribe in India, in ancient Athens or modern Rome; yet that his character is susceptible of violent changes, and becomes moulded into infinite diversities by the influence of government, climate, civilization, wealth, and poverty. By showing us how man has acted, it shows us to a certain degree how he will ever act in given circumstances; and general rules and maxims are drawn from it for the service of the lawgiver and the statesman.

It is another advantage of history, that it stores the mind with facts that apply to most

subjects which occur in conversation among
enlightened people. Whether morals, commerce, languages, or polite literature be the
object of discussion, it is history that must
supply her large storehouse of proofs and il-
lustrations.. A man or a woman may decline
without blame many subjects of literature, but
to be ignorant of history is not permitted to
any of a cultivated mind. It may be reck-
oned among its advantages, that this study
naturally increases the love of every man to
his country. We can only love what we
know; it is by becoming acquainted with the
long line of patriots, heroes, and distinguished
men, that we learn to love the country which
has produced them.

But if an acquaintance with history thus increases a rational love of our country, it also
tends to check those low, illiberal, vulgar prej-
udices which adhere to the uninformed of
every nation. Traveling will also cure them;

but to travel is not within the power of every one. There is no use, but a great deal of harm, in fostering a contempt for other nations; in an arrogant assumption of superiority, and the clownish sneer of ignorance at everything in laws, government, or manners, which is not fashioned after our partial ideas and familiar usages. A well-informed person will not be apt to exclaim at every event out of the common way that nothing like it has ever happened since the creation of the world, that such atrocities are totally unheard of in any age or nation— sentiments we have all of us so often heard of late on the subject of the French revolution ; when, in fact, we can scarcely open a page of their history without being struck with similar and equal enormities. Indeed, party spirit is very much cooled and checked by an acquaint-ance with the events of past times.

When we see the mixed and imperfect virtue of the most distinguished characters ; the variety of motives, some pure and some impure, which influence political conduct; the partial success of the wisest schemes, and the frequent failure of the fairest hopes—we shall find it more difficult to choose a side and to keep up an interest towards it in our minds, than to restrain our feelings and language within the bounds of good sense and moderation. This, by the way, makes it particularly proper that ladies who interest themselves in the events of public life should have their minds cultivated by an acquaintance with history, without which they are apt to let the whole warmth of their natures flow out upon party matters, in an ardor more honest than wise, more zealous than candid.

We have considered the uses of history; I would now direct your attention to those collateral branches of science which are necessary for the profitable understanding of it. It is impossible to understand one thing well without understanding to a certain degree many other things; there is a mutual dependence between all parts of knowledge. This is the reason that a child never fully comprehends what he is taught; he receives an idea, but not the full idea, perhaps not the principle of what you want to teach him. But as his mind opens, this idea enlarges and receives accessory ideas, till slowly and by degrees he is master of the whole. This is particularly the case in regard to the perusal of history. You may recollect probably that the mere *adventure* was all you entered into, in those portions of it which were presented to you at a very early age. You could understand nothing of the springs of action, nothing of the connection of events with the intrigues of cabinets, with religion, with commerce; nothing of the state of the world at different periods of society and improvement; and as little could you grasp the measured distances of time and space which are set between them. This you could not do, not because the history was not related with clearness, but because you were destitute of other knowledge.

The first studies which present themselves as accessories in this light are *Geography* and *Chronology*, which have been called the two eyes of history. When was it done? where was it done? are the two first questions you would ask concerning any fact that was related to you. Without these two particulars there can be no precision or clearness.

Geography is best learned along with history; for if the first explains history, the latter gives interest to geography, which without it is but a dry list of names. For this reason, if a young person begin with ancient history, I should think it advisable, after a slight general acquaintance with the globe, to confine his geography to the period and country of which he is reading; and it would

be a desirable thing to have maps adapted to
each remarkable period in the great empires
of the world. These should not contain any
towns, or be divided into any provinces, which
were not known at that period. A map of
Egypt, for instance, calculated for its ancient
monarchy, should have Memphis marked in it,
but not Alexandria, because the two capitals
did not exist together. A map of Judea for
the time of Solomon, or any period of its
monarchy, should not exhibit the name of
Samaria, nor the villages of Bethany and
Nazareth: but each country should have the
towns and divisons, as far as they are known,
calculated for the period the map was meant
to illustrate. Thus geography, civil geography, would be seen to grow out of history;
and the mere view of the map would suggest
the political state of the world at any period.

The young student should make it an in-
variable rule never to read history without a

map before him ; to which should be added plans of towns, harbors, &c. These should be conveniently placed under the eye, separate if possible from the book he is reading, that by frequent glancing upon them the image of the country may be indelibly impressed on his imagination.

Besides the necessity of maps for understanding history, the memory is wonderfully assisted by the local association which they supply. The battles of Issus and the Granicus will not be confounded by those who have taken the pains to trace the rivers on whose banks they were fought : the exploits of Hannibal are connected with a view of the Alps, and the idea of Leonidas is inseparable from the straits of Thermopylæ. The greater accuracy of maps, and still more the facility, from the arts of printing and engraving, of procuring them, is an advantage the moderns have over the ancients.

Although I recommend to you a constant attention to chronology, I do not think it desirable to load your memory with a great number of specific dates, both because it would be too great a burden on the retentive powers, and because it is, after all, not the best way of attaining clear ideas on the subjects of history. In order to do this, it is necessary to have in your mind the relative situation of other countries at the time of any event recorded in one of them. For instance, if you have got by heart the dates of the accession of the kings of Europe, and want to know whether John lived at the time of the crusades, and in what state the Greek empire was, you cannot tell without an arithmetical process, which perhaps you may not be quick enough to make. You cannot tell whether Constantinople had been taken by the Turks when the Sicilian Vespers happened ; for each fact is insulated in your mind, and indeed your dates give you only the dry catalogue of accessions. Nay you may read separate histories, and yet not bring them together, if the countries be remote. Each exists in your mind separately, and you have at no time the state of the world. But you ought to have an idea at once of the whole world, as far as history will give it. You do not see truly what the Greeks were, except you know that the British Isles were then barbarous.

A few dates, therefore, perfectly learned, may suffice, and may serve as landmarks to prevent your going far astray in the rest : but it will be highly useful to connect the histories you read in such a manner in your own mind, that you may be able to refer from one to the other, and to form them all into a whole. For this purpose, it is very desirable to observe and retain in your memory certain coincidences, which may link, as it were, two nations together. Thus you may remember that Haroun al Raschid sent to Charlemagne the first clock that was seen in Europe.   If you are reading the history of Greece when it flourished most, and want to know what the Romans were doing at the same time, you may recollect that they sent to Greece for instruction when they wanted to draw up the laws of the Twelve Tables.   Solon and Crœsus connected the history of Lesser Asia with that of Greece.   Egbert was brought up in the court of Charlemagne ; Philip Augustus of France and Richard I. of England fought in the same crusade against Saladin.   Queen Elizabeth received the French ambassador in deep mourning after the massacre of St. Bartholomew.

It may be desirable to keep one kingdom as a metre for the rest.   Take for this purpose first the Jews, then the Greeks, the Romans, and, because it is so, our own country; then harmonize and connect all the other dates with these.

That the literary history of a nation may be connected with the political, study also biography, and endeavor to link men of science and literature and artists with political characters. Thus Hippocrates was sent for to the plague of Athens; Leonardo da Vinci died in the arms of Francis I. Often an anecdote, a smart saying, will indissolubly fix a date.

Sometimes you may take a long reign, as that of Elizabeth or Louis XIV., and making that the centre, mark all the contemporary sovereigns, and also the men of letters. Another way is, to make a line of life, composed of distinguished characters who touch each other. It will be of great service to you in this view to study Dr. Priestley's biographical chart; and of still greater, to make one for yourself, and fill it by degrees as your acquaintance with history extends. Marriages connect the history of different kingdoms; as those of

Mary, Queen of Scots and Francis II.; Philip II. and Mary of England.

These are the kind of dates which make every thing lie in the mind in its proper order; they also take fast hold of it. If you forget the exact date by years, you have nothing left; but of circumstances you never lose all idea. As we come nearer to our own times, dates must be more exact; a few years more or less signify little in the destruction of Troy, if we knew it exactly; but the conclusion of the American war should be accurately known, or it will throw other events near it into confusion.

In so extensive a study no auxiliary is to be neglected; poetry impresses both geography and history in a most agreeable manner upon those who are fond of it. Thus,

——fair Austria spreads her mournful charms,
The queen, the beauty, sets the world in arms.

A short, lively character in verse is never forgotten:

From Macedonia's madman to the Swede.

Painting is a good auxiliary; and though in this country history is generally read before we see pictures, they mutually illustrate one another; painting also shows the costume. In France, where pictures are more accessible, there is more knowledge generally diffused of common history. Many have learned Scripture history from the rude figures on Dutch tiles.

I will conclude with the remark, that though the beginner in history may and ought to study dates and epochs for his guidance, chronology can never be fully possessed till after history has been long studied and carefully digested.

THE YOUNG LADY'S LIBRARY.

There is no subject on which a word of good advice is more valuable to a young lady than on the choice of books for her library. The abundance of useless and pernicious books, and the scarcity of those which may be recommended without hesitation, render it a dangerous thing for a young *lady* to read whatever may fall in her way. There are many works whose tendency is to undermine the principles and corrupt the heart; and there are others which captivate the fancy while they mislead the judgment, and present fascinating, but utterly false views of life, its purposes, pursuits, and enjoyments.

The influence exerted by such works is not the less real, because it is often imperceptible.

There are other compositions whose undoubted tendency is to delight and profit at the same time; to correct the taste, form the predilection for all that is excellent and praiseworthy, and enrich the mind with the materials of conversation and reflection, and the incitements to honorable exertion.

In those works which belong properly to the department of polite literature, the influence, whether for good or evil, is most sensibly felt, and here it is most necessary to place the young and unexperienced upon their guard.

The danger is that, in such cases, we do not discriminate the distinct action of associated causes. Even in what is presented to the senses, we are aware of the power of habitual combination. An object naturally disagreeable becomes beautiful, because we have often seen the sun shine or the dew sparkle upon it, or it has been grouped in a scene of peculiar interest. Thus the powers of fancy and of taste blend associations in the mind which disguise the original nature of moral qualities. A liberal generosity, a disinterested self-devotion, a powerful energy or deep sensibility of soul, a contempt of danger and death, are often so connected in story with the most profligate principles and manners, that the latter are excused and even sanctified by the former.

Although I have illustrated the moral influence of literature principally from its mischiefs, yet it is obvious, if what I have said be just, it may be rendered no less powerful as a means of good.   Is it not true that within the last century a decided and important improvement in the moral character of our literature has taken place? and had Pope and Smollett written at the present day, would the former have published the imitations of Chaucer, and the latter the adventures of Pickle and Random? Genius cannot now sanctify impurity or want of principle; and our critics and reviewers are exercising jurisdiction not only upon the literature, but moral blemishes of the authors that come before them. We

notice with peculiar pleasure the sentence of
just indignation which the Edinburgh tribunal
has pronounced upon Moore, Swift, Goethe,
and in general the German sentimentalists.

Indeed, the fountains of literature, into
which an enemy has sometimes infused poison,
naturally flow with refreshment and health.
Cowper and Campbell have led the muses to
repose in the bowers of religion and virtue;
and Miss Edgeworth has so cautiously combined the features of her characters, that the
predominant expression is ever what it should
be; she has shown us, not vices ennobled by
virtues, but virtues degraded and perverted by
their union with vices. The success of this
lady has been great, but had she availed herself more of the motives and sentiments of religion, we think it would have been greater.
She has stretched forth a powerful hand to the
impotent in virtue; and had she added with
the apostle, in the name of Jesus of Nazareth,

6

we should almost have expected miracles from its touch.

When the above remarks of Professor Frisbie were written, Mrs. Hemans was unknown to the American public. Had he lived to peruse her poetry, we think his testimony to its admirable moral tendency would not have been withheld. It would be no easy matter to find another votary of the muses who has done so much as this lady to elevate and ennoble the character of her own sex. Her works, with those of Mrs. Barbauld, Miss Taylor, Miss Moore, Mrs. Opie, and Miss H. Adams, may be cordially commended for their moral tendency, as well as for their literary excellence.

We mention these first, because they are female writers. In proceeding to enumerate some of the works which a careful perusal enables us to recommend without any reserve, we would by no means be understood to attempt a complete catalogue of books suitable for a young lady's reading. A small and select library is what we propose, and we shall deem ourselves fortunate if we shall succed in directing our young friends to the fountains of truly healthful literature.

MISCELLANEOUS WORKS.

Bertha's Visit to her Sister in England.

Evenings at Home. Unrivaled among works intended for young ladies.

The Lady of the Manor. By Mrs. Sherwood.

The Son of a Genius. By Mrs. Hofland.

The Library of Entertaining Knowledge.

Rasselas.

Exiles of Siberia. By Madame Cottin.

My Early Days.

Contributions of Q. Q. By Jane Taylor.

Evenings in Boston.

Oriental Anecdotes.

Anecdotes of Animals.

The Sketch Book. By Washington Irving.

HISTORY AND BIOGRAPHY.

Robertson's History of America.

Robertson's History of Scotland.

Robertson's History of Charles V.

Frost's History of Ancient and Modern Greece.

Botta's American Revolution.

Marshall's Life of Washington.

Goldsmith's History of England. [The complete work.]

Rollin's Ancient History.

Scott's History of Scotland.

Scott's Tales of a Grandfather.

Plutarch's Lives.

˙Irving's Conquest of Grenada.

Irving's Life of Columbus.

Life of John Ledyard.

Life of Patrick Henry.

Redwood. By Miss Sedgwick.

Alison on Taste.

The Spectator.

The Rambler.

Paul and Virginia.

Our Village. By Miss Mitford.

Wirt's British Spy.

MORAL AND RELIGIOUS WORKS.

Chalmers's Works.
Extracts from Fenelon's Works.
Massillon's Sermons.
Bourdaloue's Sermons.
Harbaugh's Works.
Taylor's Holy Living.
Taylor's Holy Dying.
Taylor's Life of Christ.
Baxter's Call.
Law's Serious Call.
William Penn's Works.
Paley's Works.
Dick's Christian Philosopher.
Dick's Philosophy of a Future State.
Dick's Philosophy of Religion.
Alexander, Watson, Jenyns, Leslie, and Paley's Evidences of Christianity: in one pocket volume.

These writers are of various Christian denominations, but they all agree in eloquently urging upon us the great duties of religion and morality.

POETRY.

Milton's Poems.
Cowper's Poems.
Walter Scott's Poems.
Campbell's Poems.
Dana's Poems.
Bryant's Poems.
Wilson's Poems.
Southey's Poems.
Wordsworth's Poems.
Bowles's Poems.
Coleridge's Poems.
Kirke White's Poems.
Barnard Barton's Poems.
Milman's Poems.
Hillhouse's Poems, viz. Hadad and Percy's Masque.

TRAVELS.

Irving's Voyages and Discoveries of the Companions of Columbus.

The Modern Traveler.

Heber's Travels in India.

A Year in Spain. By a Young American. A most delightful book.

Adventures and Discoveries in Africa.

Voyages and Discoveries in Polar Regions.

The last two volumes form a part of Harper's Family Library.

Many publications of light reading intended merely to amuse, not instruct, are worthless and pernicious.

But suitable and important as these and many other books are for the perusal of any person, there is one that is superior to them all; a book that has been preferred above all others by the wisest and best persons of either sex—by ministers and all worthy members of all evangelical denominations, by the most erudite scholars of all nations, by men of the most gigantic intellects, such as Isaac Newton and Sir William Jones, and was preferred above all other books by Miss Miller—and that book is the Bible, which we advise all persons to read thoroughly, systematically and devoutly. It contains the most valuable in-

struction on the most important subject.   It
has been given to us as a lamp to our feet and
a light to our path

" While marching through Immanuel's land
To fairer worlds on high."

The celebrated bard of Avon has left us the
following lofty poetic thoughts on death:

To die—to sleep—
No more: and by a sleep to say we end
The heartache, and the thousand natural shocks
That flesh is heir to—'tis a consummation
Devoutly to be wish'd :—to die—to sleep—
To sleep ! perchance to dream, aye, there's the rub.
For in that sleep of death what dreams may come,
When we have shuffled off this mortal coil,
Must give us pause.   There's the respect
That makes calamity of so long life :
For who would bear the whips and scorns of time,
The oppressor's wrong, the proud man's contumely,
The pangs of despised love, the law's delay,
The insolence of officers, and the spurns ·
That patient merit of the unworthy takes,
But that the dread of something after death
(That undiscovered country from whose bourne
No traveler returns) puzzles the will
And makes us rather bear the ills we have
Than fly to others that we know not of.

We now close by the addition of the following sentiment: Mental culture should always be made conducive to moral advancement ; the best emotions of the heart should be cherished at all times; as there is nothing so well adapted to the welfare of all classes of any age as true Christianity.

Having given a brief narrative of the leading incidents and noble examples of one whose peculiar merits attracted attention, and secured esteem during her life-time, and digested them as a manual for those who may appreciate them, it remains for us to take leave of our readers, with the fervent hope that a perusal of this small volume may be accompanied by the divine blessing, and thus contribute to the cause of education and pure piety.

Everything external is hastening to change and dissolution. You yourselves are gliding insensibly down the current of time. Can you bear the thought of resigning your passage to eternity to the blind impulse of chance, caprice and ignorance? Or can you, like illiterate and incurious mariners, sailing by some beautiful coast, be satisfied to hurry along, without attending to the various prospects and numerous objects, which nature and art have spread out before you; or without taking advantage of the best assistance you can find on your voyage, to improve whatever is instructive, or ornamental and praiseworthy? Have you forgotten, that when landed on the blissful shore your felicity will bear no inconsiderable proportion to your present attainments in knowledge; that the most enlarged understandings, where the dispositions have been of a piece, will be rewarded by the noblest discoveries; in short, that they who shine now in the fairest lights of wisdom, shall, like the more distinguishing stars of heaven, be crowned hereafter with superior splendor!

The scenes of nature contribute powerfully to inspire that serenity which heightens their beauties, and is necessary to our full enjoyment of them.   By a secret sympathy, the soul catches the harmony which it contemplates, and the frame within assimilates itself to that without.   In this state of sweet composure we become susceptible of virtuous impressions from almost every surrounding object.

But the taste for natural beauty is subservient to higher purposes than those which have been enumerated.   The cultivation of it not only refines and humanizes, but dignifies and exalts the affections.   It elevates them to the admiration and love of that Being, who is the Author of all that is fair, sublime and good in the creation.   Skepticism and irreligion are hardly compatible with the sensibility of heart which arises from a just and lively relish of the wisdom, harmony and order subsisting in the world around us. Emotions of piety must spring up spontaneously in the bosom that is in unison with all animated nature. Actuated by this beneficial and divine inspiration, man finds a fane in every grove; and, glowing with devout fervor, he joins his song to the universal chorus, or muses the praise of the Almighty in more expressive silence.

No character commands more respect than that of the religious and cultivated woman; and it is to the credit of the sex that letters and religion have usually been associated. We dwell with pleasure on the piety of Lady Jane Grey, if that of Elizabeth be questionable. And we may surely hope that she, who, when copies of the Scriptures were still scarce, presented the Hebrew Pentateuch to a scholar too poor to buy one, could herself appreciate the sacred gift. Neither can we forget more recent examples. The names of Russell, and of Hutchinson, of Rowe, Chapone and Smith,

of the amiable authoress of Father Clement,
and of the revered Hannah More, are together
treasured in our minds.

HYMN.

FOR THE CLOSE OF A SABBATH-SCHOOL.

When shall we thus meet again ?
When shall we thus meet again ?
When the dreary winter's past,
When is hushed the northern blast,
When new verdure clothes the plain,
Then may we here meet again.

But what changes first may come !
Of our happy number, some,
Round a much-loved parent's bier,
May let fall the parting tear ;
And in orphan grief complain,
Ere we thus shall meet again.

Of our little blooming band,
Some may feel death's icy hand ;
From the friends on earth we love,
Early make our long remove ;
And among this favored train,
Never, never meet again !

Or, perhaps the fatal dart
May some faithful teacher's heart
Pierce, with death's dissolving throes;
And those lips in silence close,
Which have made our duty plain,
Ere we thus shall meet again.

Let us then with care improve
Lessons taught in Christian love;
Let each truth their lips impart
Dwell in every grateful heart;
That—their labors not in vain—
We at last may meet again.

When our summers all have fled—
When the task of life is said—
When our wasting years shall be
Lost in vast eternity—
Where the "saints immortal reign"—
Then may we *all* meet again!

SEMINARY HYMN.

BY S. L. C.

Brothers, hark! the Lord is calling,
　He has work for us to do;
Long our comrades have been toiling,
　Shall we prove to them untrue?

See ! the distant light is breaking,
  Let us put our armor on ;
When the Master calls for waking,
  Should we tarry for the morn ?

'Tis no time for us to slumber,
  For the precious moments fly ;
Hear those voices without number,
  Crying, " Save us ere we die !"
We can lead them to the fountain,
  Where the healing waters flow ;
We can point them to the mountain,
  Where a refuge they may know.

Shall we shrink from toil or danger,
  Fearing that we'll faint or die ?
It is God who gives our armor,
  Then there's naught can terrify.
God our life ! and God our leader !
  Need we lay our banners down ?
Surely He will strengthen ever,
  And at last will give a crown.

Holy Father, be thou near us,
  Here we pledge to Thee our all ;
Take us, use us, blessed Jesus,
  We will follow at Thy call.
May the presence of the Spirit,
  With all grace our bosoms fill ;
Thine the glory, Thine the merit,
  Ours the love to do Thy will.

I CAME TO THE PLACE WHERE MY CHILD-
HOOD HAD DWELT.

BY REV. JAMES GILBOURNE LYONS, LL. D.

I came to the place where my childhood had dwelt,
To the hearth where in early devotion I knelt ;—
The fern and the bramble grew wild in the hall,
And the long grass of summer wav'd green on the
     wall :
The roof-tree was fallen, the household had fled,
The garden was ruin'd, the roses were dead,
The wild bird flew scar'd from her desolate stone,
And I breath'd in the home of my boyhood—alone.

That moment is past, but it left on my heart
A remembrance of sadness which will not depart ;—
I have wander'd afar since that wonderful day,
I have wept with the mournful, and laugh'd with the
     gay ;
I have lived with the stranger, and drunk of the rills
Which have warbled their music on loftier hills ;
But I never forgot, in rejoicing or care,
That mouldering hearth, and those hills of Lazare.

Yet droop not, my spirit, nor hopelessly mourn
Over ills which the best and the wisest have borne ;—
Though the greetings of love, and the voices of mirth,
May for ever be hush'd in the homesteads of earth ;

Though the dreams and the dwellings of childhood
  decay,
And the friends whom we cherish go hasting away,
No young hopes e'er are scatter'd, no heart-strings
  are riven,
No partings are known in the households of Heaven.

———

While very young Henrietta learned some
favorite hymns that she soon sang with delightful effect. Instances:

  " Oh the hope, the joyful hope,
      The hope that Jesus gives ;
      The hope when days and years are passed,
      We all shall meet in Heaven at last,
      Where sorrow shall be o'er."

" Work for the Night is Coming," " Your
Mission," "Sweet Hour of Prayer," "Cali-
fornia Brothers," solo—" I am Weary," " A
beautiful land of rest I see, a land of rest
from sorrow free."

As an evidence of her surprising aptness in
committing to memory, her Pa presented her
with a book containing Pope's Universal

Prayer, when she was between six and seven years old, with the promise of another book when she would learn that prayer by heart, supposing it would require a week or longer, as it contains fifty-two lines. But being pleased with the offer, and accustomed to a cordial compliance with the wishes of her parents, she commenced the task, and on the third day was able to repeat it all without mistake. The same is here inserted to encourage other youths to do so likewise.

THE UNIVERSAL PRAYER.

Father of all, in every age,
  In every clime adored;
By saint, by savage and by sage,
  Jehovah, Jove or Lord.
Thou great first cause, least understood;
  To all my sense confined,
To know but this, that thou art good,
  And that myself am blind.
Yet gave me in this dark estate,
  To see the good from ill;
And binding nature fast in fate,
  Left free the human will.

What conscience dictates to be done,
　Or warns me not to do,
This teach me more than Hell to shun,
　That more than Heaven pursue ;
What blessings thy free bounty gives,
　Let me not cast away ;
For God is paid when man receives,
　To enjoy is to obey ;
Yet not to earth's contracted span,
　Thy goodness let me bound,
Or think thee Lord alone of man
　When thousand worlds are round.
Let not this weak unknowing hand,
　Presume thy bolts to throw ;
Nor deal damnation round the land,
　On each I judge thy foe,
If I am right thy grace impart
　Still in the right to stay ;
If I am wrong, oh teach my heart,
　To find the better way.
Save me alike from foolish pride,
　Or impious discontent ;
At aught thy wisdom had denied,
　Or aught thy goodness lent.
Teach me to feel another's woe,
　To hide the faults I see,
The mercy I to others show,
　That mercy show to me.

Mean—though I am not wholly so,
 Since quickened by thy grace,
O lead me wheresoe'er I go,
 Through this day's life or death.
This day be bread and peace my lot,
 All else beneath the sun,
Thou knowest if best bestowed or not,
 And let thy will be done.
To thee whose Temple is all space,
 Whose Altar—earth, sea, skies,
One chorus let all beings raise,
 All nature's incense rise.

SOLO:

[Sung by Miss Vanleer, a pupil of Miss Miller's, at a S. S. concert, May, 1874.]

1. I'm weary, I'm fainting, my day's work is done,
 I'm watching and waiting for life's setting sun ;
 The shadows are stretching afar o'er the lea ;
 Then oh ! let me anchor beyond the dark sea.

2. The cold surging billows that break at my feet,
 Have lost all their terror, their music is sweet ;
 My Saviour is stilling the tempest for me ;
 Then oh ! let me anchor beyond the dark sea.

3. Come, loving Redeemer, and take to thy breast,
The heart that is panting and sighing for rest;
My Saviour, I'm waiting, I'm waiting for thee;
Then oh! let me anchor beyond the dark sea.

4. I'll lay my life's burden, O Lord, at thy feet,
For loved ones are watching my spirit to greet.
The portals of glory are open for me
Then oh! let me anchor beyond the dark sea.

One of the hymns that Henrietta learned by heart when she was about seven years old, and became fond of singing was

1. Hail! sweetest, dearest tie that binds
Our glowing hearts in one!
Hail! sacred hope that tunes our minds,
To harmony divine!

Chorus—

It is the hope, the blissful hope,
Which Jesus' grace has given,
The hope when days and years are past,
We all shall meet in heaven.
We all shall meet in heaven at last—
We all shall meet in heaven:
The hope when days and years are past,
We all shall meet in heaven.

2. What though the northern wintry blast
    Shall howl around thy cot;
What though beneath an eastern sun,
    Be cast our distant lot ;
        Yet still we share the blissful hope, etc.

3. From Burmah's shores from Afric's strand,
    From India's burning plain,
From Europe, from Columbia's land
    We hope to meet again.
        It is the hope, the blissful hope, etc.

4. No lingering look, no parting sigh,
    Our future meeting knows ;
There friendship beams from every eye,
    And hope immortal grows.
            O sacred hope ! O blissful hope !
            Which Jesus' grace has given, etc.

The following Hymn was a favorite of Miss Miller's, that she often sung accompanied on the melodeon with much effect :

"THE HOUR OF PRAYER."

1. Sweet hour of prayer ! sweet hour of prayer !
    That calls me from a world of care,
    And bids me at my Father's throne
    Make all my wants and wishes known;
    In seasons of distress and grief,

My soul has often found relief;
And oft escaped the tempter's snare
By thy return, sweet hour of prayer,
And oft escaped the tempter's snare
By thy return, sweet hour of prayer.

2. Sweet hour of prayer! sweet hour of prayer!
Thy wings shall my petition bear,
To Him whose truth and faithfulness,
Engage the waiting soul to bless ;
And since He bids me seek His face,
Believe His word and trust His grace,
I'll cast on Him my every care,
And wait for thee, sweet hour of prayer.

3. Sweet hour of prayer! sweet hour of prayer!
May I thy consolation share ;
Till, from Mount Pisgah's lofty height,
I view my home and take my flight;
This robe of flesh I'll drop, and rise
To seize the everlasting prize,
And shout, while passing through the air,
Farewell, farewell, sweet hour of prayer.

This hymn Henrietta learned by heart and
often sung early in the morning while she was
a little girl.

ALICE CARY'S DYING HYMN.

Earth, with its dark and dreadful ills,
  Recedes and fades away ;
Lift up your heads, ye heavenly hills,
  Ye gates of death give way !

My soul is full of whispering song;
  My blindness is my sight.
The shadows that I feel so long
  Are still alive with light.

That while my pulses faintly beat,
  My faith does so abound,
I feel grow firm beneath my feet
  The green, immortal ground.

That faith to me a courage gives,
  Low as the grave to go ;
I know that my Redeemer lives—
  That I shall live I know.

The palace walls I almost see
  Where dwells my Lord and King.
O grave ! where is thy victory ?
  O death ! where is thy sting ?

Who would not brave the swelling tide,
Of earthly toil and care,
To wake on high when life is past,
Over the stream at home at last,
With all the blest ones there,
With all the blest ones there.